THE ARSENAL STADIUM MYSTERY

LEONARD GRIBBLE

With an Introduction by
MARTIN EDWARDS

BRITISH LIBRARY

This edition published 2018 by
The British Library
96 Euston Road
London NW1 2DB

Originally published in 1939 by George G. Harrap & Co. Ltd., London
© 1939 Leonard Gribble
Introduction copyright © 2018 Martin Edwards

Cataloguing in Publication Data
A catalogue record for this book is available from the British Library

ISBN 978 0 7123 5226 0

Typeset by Tetragon, London
Printed and bound by CPI Group (UK) Ltd, Croydon CRO 4YY

THE ARSENAL
STADIUM MYSTERY

INTRODUCTION

The Arsenal Stadium Mystery is an unusual and historically significant whodunit first published in 1939. The story features Leonard
Gribble's series detective Inspector Slade, and in some respects is
a typical "fair play" mystery of the type so popular during "the
Golden Age of Murder" between the two world wars. But it's
highly distinctive, for three reasons. First, the storyline focuses on
professional football, a sport seldom featured, or even mentioned,
in crime novels of the era. Second, it features a large supporting
cast of characters well-known from real life—the manager and
players of Arsenal Football Club. And third, it began life as a serial
in the *Daily Express*, with the book version treated from the outset
as a "film tie-in".

The dust jacket blurb for the first edition hailed the book as
Gribble's "most original detective story... With the co-operation
of Mr George Allison, secretary-manager of the Arsenal F.C.,
and of the players... Leonard Gribble has been given facilities
for writing an entirely new kind of mystery—one which takes
the reader behind the scenes of the most famous football club
in the world. Here is big-time football as seen from the inside;
here are the national Soccer stars introduced as they really are.
A well-known footballer drops dead... murdered before 70,000
witnesses..." The victim, one hastens to add, is not an Arsenal
player, but a member of a fictitious team of amateurs called the
Trojans.

The front cover and spine of the dust jacket was devoted to a photograph of George Allison and his players discussing tactics with the aid of a football board game.The rear cover of the jacket featured a photograph of Gribble and the actor Leslie Banks, and recounted a supposed conversation between them about the film of the book, in which Banks played Inspector Slade. The film, light-hearted and pacy, was directed by Thorold Dickinson, whom Martin Scorsese described as "one of the most ambitious and talented film-makers of his time"; Scorsese admired the film, and was quoted by Philip Horne in an article for *The Daily Telegraph* in 2005 as saying "even as someone who can't stand sports—soccer, anything with a ball—I find the soccer scenes exhilarating". Graham Greene was another fan of the film, praising Dickinson's "wit of cutting and wit of angle".

Banks plays Slade as something of an eccentric, who wears a different hat in every scene. In Gribble's books, Slade is a less striking character, no doubt intended as a more realistic figure than Great Detectives such as Hercule Poirot, Lord Peter Wimsey, and the Oxford-educated gentlemanly cops created by authors including Ngaio Marsh and Michael Innes. In the film, George Allison has a speaking part, unlike the Arsenal players. The football action scenes were mostly shot on the ground of Brentford Football Club, while the music was written by a composer at the start of his film career. Miklos Rosza would in later years receive three Academy Awards, and compose soundtracks for films such as *Ben Hur* and *El Cid*.

The book, like the film, can be enjoyed even by football-phobic mystery fans who don't know their Arsenal Stadium from their Elland Road. This is because Gribble switches suspicion quite effectively between members of a small group of people who might have a motive to kill the victim, a businessman and notorious philanderer. For the modern soccer enthusiast, part of the fascination of the story is that it shines a light on "the beautiful game" during a very different time, long before Arsenal finally decamped from Highbury Stadium, and marketed the naming rights of their majestic new ground to Emirates Airlines.

It was an era when the central conceit of the story, that a team of English amateurs could compete on more or less equal terms with Arsenal, did not require excessive suspension of disbelief. Indeed, Bernard Joy, Arsenal's centre half, who appears in the story, was a school teacher by profession, and the last amateur to play football for England's national side. In 1939, the idea of footballers becoming pampered multi-millionaires, and football teams being so dominated by overseas stars that the ruling bodies would find themselves forced to legislate to require a minimum quota of "homegrown" players in each club squad would have seemed absurd.

In the age of Twitter frenzies and blog tours, it's tempting to assume that an unashamedly commercial approach to marketing a book is a modern phenomenon. But *The Arsenal Stadium Mystery* is an example (and by no means the only one) of a Golden Age detective novel that benefited from a shrewd and imaginative approach to the business of bookselling. The page facing the first page of Chapter One was even devoted to facsimiles of the autographs of the Arsenal players.

Much of the credit for this was surely due to the author himself. Leonard Reginald Gribble (1908–85) is not perhaps a name to conjure with, although it prompted the distinguished critic H.R.F. Keating to feature him in an essay about prolific crime writers

titled "Scribble, Scribble, Mr Gribble". Certainly, Gribble's fame
does not match that of illustrious contemporaries such as Agatha
Christie, Dorothy L. Sayers, or even Freeman Wills Crofts. But he
was a capable writer with a highly professional approach to his
craft, and he knew how to make the most of his talents.

Born in Barnstaple, he started publishing detective stories—
the first was *The Case of the Marsden Rubies* (1929)—in his early
twenties, and kept writing for rather more than half a century. A
hard-working author, he produced so many books that he found
it necessary to adopt a host of pen-names: Leo Grex, Sterry
Browning, James Gannett, Louis Grey, Piers Marlowe, Dexter Muir,
and Bruce Sanders. Although his main focus was on mysteries, his
varied output included westerns and non-fiction. Gribble's energy
matched that of another highly prolific novelist, John Creasey,
who established the Crime Writers' Association in 1953. Gribble
was an obvious choice to become a founder member, and he and
Creasey became good friends.

The Arsenal Stadium Mystery remains his most celebrated book.
Ironically, the Government commandeered Highbury Stadium
during the Second World War, and Nancy Frost (daughter of one
of the club's directors, Ralph Fielder) recalled many years later
watching "home" games at White Hart Lane, the ground of
Arsenal's rivals, Tottenham Hotspur. She prized her copy of the
first edition which included a page of actual (rather than facsimile)
autographs of the Arsenal team of 1942, with elegant calligraphy
courtesy of Bernard Joy.

In 1950 (when he also produced *They Kidnapped Stanley Matthews*,
featuring an English soccer legend), Gribble published an updated
version of his most popular book—*The Arsenal Stadium Mystery:
a Replay*. The first edition came complete with a wrap-around

promotional band bearing an encomium from Bernard Joy (who was by then a journalist) and is in itself now a sought-after collector's item. Both books have long been out of print, but the appearance of the British Library edition means that modern readers now have a chance to enjoy a slice of sporting nostalgia as well as pitting their wits against Inspector Slade's.

MARTIN EDWARDS
www.martinedwardsbooks.com

Arsenal autographs, 1939

I

History Is Made at Highbury

THERE WAS A SUDDEN, EXPECTANT HUSH AS TOM WHITTAKER walked into the dressing-room of the Arsenal team at Highbury, that same hush he has been greeted with for years, on every Arsenal home-match day.

"The boss wants to see you all upstairs in a quarter of an hour," he announced.

"O.K., Tom."

"Sure."

"Righto, Tom."

Life, suspended for a few moments for the almost traditional announcement, flowed again. The eleven first-team players idling in the dressing-room, waiting for the time when they can start changing, picked up the scraps of conversation they had let fall when the trainer entered.

One of the trainer's assistants, standing by a table near the door into the main corridor, continued with his task of quartering a lemon. He let the knife he was using rattle against the table's top. On to a cracked plate he poured a pile of sugar-coated squares of chewing gum.

"Just what I was looking for," said a soft Welsh voice.

A couple of the chewing-gum squares disappeared behind Bryn Jones's white teeth.

The assistant might not have heard or noticed. He was whistling under his breath, and seemed intent on the tune.

"Hey, Bryn, what did you draw in the sweep?"

Britain's highest-priced soccer star turned to satisfy the curiosity of his namesake from Aberdare. Leslie Jones's round face was frowning reflectively. Beside him sat Bremner, on a seat that extended round three of the white-tiled walls. The forward was watching Swindin as the goalkeeper sat contemplating the green squares of the floor.

"What's the matter?" he called, causing the goalkeeper to look up and grin.

"He's looking for the double six," said Ted Drake, his full-toned Hampshire voice pleasant to the ear.

"And looks like he's only got the double blank," chimed in Jack Crayston, brushing his curly hair with his left hand.

There was a general laugh from those in earshot. The speakers were well known for the strong domino school they formed on the journeys to away matches.

Light banter was flung to and fro, like a practice ball, but it was all on the surface, concealing each man's true thoughts, masking his real feelings; and somehow it did not quite rob the atmosphere of tension, which was reflected in the earnestness on Cliff Bastin's face as he read the team lists on the notice-board, in the slightly nervous gesture of Bernard Joy's hands as he fingered his "lucky" tie, in the springy motions of Eddie Hapgood as he argued some point with his team partner George Male, and turned to throw a word at Alf Kirchen, the muscular winger.

The droning whistle of the assistant at the table near the door changed key as he set out a dozen cups and piled loaf sugar on to a plate.

That last tense quarter of an hour of inaction passed slowly. There was an audible sigh of relief when Whittaker said, "All right, lads, upstairs."

The eleven members of that day's "first" team filed through a narrow door, trooped up a flight of stairs, passed along a wide corridor, and entered a comfortably furnished room where George Allison—the "boss" to every player on the Arsenal Football Club's books—was waiting, hands in trousers pockets, keen eyes watchful under contracted brows.

When the door was closed and the men had ranged themselves before the shining desk, the clear, modulated voice known to millions of sport-lovers all over the British Isles spoke.

"To-day," George Allison told the team that only the previous season had won the soccer crown, "you're going to play an historic match. You're going to stand representative, as it were, of the best qualities of professional football in this country. You're going to play the Trojans, the finest amateur side in Great Britain, the team that has captured the national imagination because of its clean, clever play. Now, I'm not going to tell you how to play. You know that. I'm just going to ask you to remember two things."

He paused, searched the faces turned towards him.

"First," he added, "not to let down the game. Second, not to let down your club. I don't ask anything else of you."

The quiet, measured tones stopped. From an open box on his desk the speaker took a Turkish cigarette and fitted it into a holder.

Softly, as from a great distance, came the muted strains of a band playing to the thousands of spectators filling the stands. Outside the Stadium it was a bright, keen day, one of those invigorating Saturdays when the lion and the lamb of March seem content with each other's company. Tawny sunshine, brittle as thin glass in the fresh but not boisterous wind, touched the fresh green of the field's turf with pale gilt.

On one or two corners those standing stamped their feet, but more from good-natured impatience than from cold. The seventy-odd thousand that had jam-packed themselves into the Stadium ground were a holiday crowd, and the way they sang the popular choruses played by the band left no doubt as to the altitude of their spirits.

They had come to see a football game that would make history, the friendly clash between the League Champions and the amateur team that had, in a surprisingly short space, captured for itself much of the glory of the old-time Corinthians. Whatever happened, they would see a keen game, a worthy struggle.

The crowd knew that, and the knowledge was balm to its impatience.

Meanwhile, in the visitors' dressing-room, Francis Kindilett, the proud manager of the Trojans, echoed the feelings expressed by George Allison to the Arsenal players.

"You're up against the stiffest proposition you've ever tackled," he told his team. "A professional side with a great record, a great tradition, and, above all, a great spirit to win. Do your best, boys. I can't ask more of you, but I'm personally confident that your best is good enough. That's all—and good luck."

He nodded to the Trojan trainer, George Raille, to take over, and opened his copy of the red-covered programme. It was a great moment for him as he read the line-up of the teams; in a way, the fulfilment of a dream. For several years he had worked hard, in season and out, to prove that Britain could produce an amateur team capable of ranking with the best of the country's professional elevens. He had done it. His team of carpenters and electricians, chemists and insurance brokers, clerks and salesmen had justified the boasts he had made.

And now the men of Troy, in their blue shirts, with the white horse on the chest, were matched against the red-and-white shirts of the Arsenal.

There was a slight mist before his eyes as he read through the teams again:

ARSENAL

Swindin

	Male		Hapgood	
	Crayston	Bernard Joy		Leslie Jones
Kirchen	Bremner	Drake	Bryn Jones	Bastin

Garrow	Wellock	Bredge	Jeuner	Setchley
	Smith	Chulley	Doyce	
	Crieff		Morring	
		Torburn		

TROJANS

He knew in his heart that, whatever the outcome of the day's battle—and that battle would be spirited, hard-fought—the men of Troy would not be disgraced. Manager Kindilett was comforted by a great confidence in his team's will-to-win.

At half-past two the Stadium was a hive of bustle and serious activity.

In the dressing-rooms freshly laundered shirts, shorts, and socks were taken from pegs. Players tried on boots, kicked the front studs against the heated green-tiled floor, to make them fit comfortably, oiled their limbs, padded their socks with cotton-wool lashed tight with rolls of bandage.

Tom Whittaker, a serious expression on his face, drew a bandage round Bastin's left ankle, another round Leslie Jones's right ankle, and found time to look at Swindin's arm—that unfortunate left arm that, shortly before Christmas, had been snapped by a kick from Hapgood in a grim tussle with Manchester United.

George Raille, alert, intent, worked hard in the visitors' dressing-room, offering a word of advice here, massaging a limb there. He stopped before Doyce, the right half, who had joined the Trojans only a week before, and was the least-known quantity in the team.

"Don't forget, Doyce. Feed your forwards. Keep up, and keep attacking."

The right half's face—handsome in an effeminate way—changed expression, became sulky, obdurate.

"You don't have to teach me twice times two, Raille."

There was a deliberate sneer to the words, but the trainer passed on, his under lip caught between his teeth. Morring, the large-framed right back, who had watched the scene, drew closer to Doyce. He was in socks and shorts, and his hairy chest had the tautness of a drum.

"For God's sake snap out of it!" he said. "Don't go on the field carrying a chip on your shoulder."

For a moment the two men eyed each other with acknowledged bitterness.

"Go to hell!" muttered Doyce, turning away.

Morring went back to his seat and took his shirt from the peg. There was a hard, inscrutable look in his eyes.

Six minutes later the crowd of more than seventy thousand roared itself hoarse as the teams ran on to the field.

"Here they come!"

"Up the Gunners!"

"Come on the Trojans! Troy! Troy!"

The shouting died, wavered like surf dragging on a shingly beach, then swelled to the roar of foaming breakers as Chulley and Hapgood, the two captains, bent over a coin spun by the referee and the former pointed to the southern goal. Troy had won the toss.

The teams lined up. Drake stood with the ball at rest against his right foot. The referee glanced up the field, taking in the crowded stands, the positioned players, the hovering linesmen, and raised the whistle to his mouth.

As its shrill note swept across the field the Arsenal centre-forward lifted the ball to his right, and Bremner pounced on it, turned, and raced forward. As the blue-shirted Smith ran in to tackle close the ball ran truly to Kirchen, who paused only to steady it, then was away.

The quick-moving, progressive advance brought a shout from the crowd. The game was on.

Every eye watched as Arsenal made that first lunge goalwards, clean, deft, sure, as though they were going to hammer flat the Trojan defence.

But that defence was malleable. The hammer-blow was hard, calculated and timed, but it made no impression. Clever co-ordination of Crieff and Chulley left Torburn free to strut between his posts, swinging his long arms.

The crowd had received their first clear impression of the play. Professional and amateur, the teams were evenly matched. There was every prospect of the struggle becoming Olympic.

Then happened one of those hazards of football that frequently upset form and players. With Troy returning the pressure, and

Bredge and Setchley giving Hapgood and Joy plenty of work, the ball suddenly ran loose in mid-field, where the watchful Bryn Jones snapped it up, like a gift from the soccer gods. Five foot six of scheming wizardry retained possession of the ball, swept it back towards the Trojan half, and released it in a long cross-drive to the waiting Drake.

Chulley was alive to the danger, and rushed to do battle, but the Arsenal centre-forward had secured a valuable half-second, due to Bryn Jones's perfect timing, and had raced through, with the Trojan centre-half in close pursuit.

Another roar rose from the thousands of throats, ringed the field.

Torburn came out of his goal, hunched like a fighter, elbows back and braced, reducing the shooting angle offered to the Arsenal forward. Chulley appeared to leap in the air, but Drake's right foot had pushed out suddenly, lifting the ball, and sending it flying across the goal, with the racing Morring unable to do anything to impede him.

Valiantly the Trojan goalkeeper flung himself upward and sideways in a desperate effort to get his fingers to the catapulted ball, but his hand was inches from it as it shot past him and landed just inside the far goal-post.

"Goal!"

"Good old Ted!"

Bredge kicked off, and the game went on. But somehow that quick, snap goal seemed to upset the Trojan machine, slowed it down. Good football was played, but the play always returned to a mid-field scramble. The remainder of that first half never attained the playing peak of those early minutes. Raids by both sides were broken up, smothered, Doyce playing a strong defensive game for the Trojans, Hapgood and Joy allowing no roving forward scope in the Arsenal area. When the whistle blew, at half-past three, the score was still 1–0 in Arsenal's favour.

As the teams filed through the glass-enclosed trainers' stand and along the corridor to their respective dressing-rooms one of the commissionaires caught the Trojan trainer's attention.

"This package was brought by District Messenger about a quarter of an hour ago," he said, handing Raille a brown-paper parcel addressed to Doyce.

"All right," said the trainer. "I'll take it in. Thanks."

In the dressing-room he gave the package to Doyce, who was sucking a piece of lemon.

"For you. Came by District Messenger."

He handed over the package and passed on. The right half frowned, scrutinized the inked address, and tore off the wrapping-paper. No one paid any attention to him. Raille was rubbing Setchley's leg with liniment and advising Bredge on how to scheme a successful raid on the Arsenal goal immediately after the kick-off.

In the Arsenal dressing-room Tom Whittaker was giving his charges some advice. But he was smiling, and there was a good measure of chaff with his seeded words. There had been no first-half *débâcle*. The amateurs had been held.

"Hold them after the kick-off, lads," he wound up. "Ten to one they'll start off with a rush. But hold them."

He was right. When Troy kicked off there was no mistaking their purpose. They were out to raid the Arsenal goal and put the count level.

Wellock, the fast-moving inside left, came up from playing a defensive game, kicked the ball away from a scramble, and ran forward with it. Beating his man, he drove the ball hard across to

Setchley, on the far wing. The winger, with clever anticipation, had placed himself well. As the ball shot across to him he alighted on it with the precision of a gull snatching a crumb. A twist of his foot, and the ball was steadied. A touch, and he was away.

But the watchful Leslie Jones was not idle. The Arsenal left half rushed forward to encounter, only to find Setchley ready for him. With a beautiful body swerve he avoided the wing stopper, and turned in. Bredge, who had moved up, was also ready, hovering for a pass.

A low, grass-cutting drive sent the ball to the centre-forward's waiting feet. Bredge turned to the right, advancing, well aware that Bernard Joy was bearing down on him, prepared to wreck a fine forward movement and to smother his advance. But Bredge was a schemer. He had held that forward line together for months, and he worked like part of a perfectly timed machine. He appeared to dawdle, and the crowd caught its breath.

Shouts of "Get on with it!" rose.

Then a swift side-swerve carried the nimble centre-forward round the Arsenal centre-half. Clear of that looming menace, Bredge did not hesitate.

He sent in a smashing first-timer.

It was a beautiful shot, but Swindin's keen eyes saw its flight, and the goalkeeper's hands got to the ball, but he could not hold it. Hapgood, playing his customary back-on-the-line defence, dropped back as the goalkeeper made an effort to retrieve the still travelling ball.

But the luck was Troy's.

Bredge, following up his first shot, got his foot to the ball again, with Swindin out of position. Again the ball sailed towards the yawning net. It would have been a certain goal but for Hapgood's right fist. Unable to get head or foot to the ball, the left back punched it over the cross-bar.

As the whistle blew for the penalty kick the shouts of the crowd were deafening.

"Come on the Trojans!"

"Troy! Troy!"

But there was sudden silence as Chulley, the Trojan captain, placed the ball for Doyce to take the penalty kick. Between the goal-posts Swindin crouched, tense as a cougar, eyes on the ball.

Doyce took a short run, and the ball rose as though released by a powerful spring. Swindin leapt like a salmon from a stream, but he had no real chance against a ball that was travelling with eye-defeating speed from the instant it left the Trojan sharp-shooter's foot.

"Goal!"

"It is!"

"Troy! Troy!"

One all.

The crowd was roused. The amateurs had staved off a threatening rot. They were now fighting like worthy challengers of champions. The crowd was reassured. This was going to be a full ninety-minute game.

The teams lined up again. As the whistle blew Drake flicked the ball to Bryn Jones, who sent it sharply across to Bremner. The Arsenal forward line went goalwards with a bound, forced a breach in the Trojan half-back line, only to find the amateurs' rearguard sound, dependable. A long kick from Crieff sent the ball dropping to the feet of a Trojan forward, who trapped it neatly, and shot away.

Necks in the stands craned eagerly forward. It was a break-away. Would it be a second Trojan goal? Had the amateurs really found their match-winning form?

However, before the Trojan forwards could position themselves for another raiding swoop on the Arsenal defence the referee's whistle shrilled.

Back in mid-field Doyce, the Trojan right half who had shot the penalty goal, lay doubled up.

Raille, in his hand a dripping sponge and a clean towel, ran out. The crowd, silent, wondering, watched as a brief consultation was held over the prone player. But something serious had happened. Doyce made no attempt to get up. He lay there, making no movement.

The crowd realized that he was out of the game, and a murmur like a new-sprung breeze wafted round the ground.

A stretcher was brought on to the field. Players crowded round as Doyce was lifted on to it. When the stretcher-bearers moved away with the game's casualty a sudden wave of hand-clapping circled the field. Doyce had played strongly in the first half, and he had scored for the amateurs.

The crowd, sporty, fair in its judgment, was giving the injured man his due.

The referee's whistle returned the remaining players to the game, and again the ball rose in a swift arc. But the murmur of the crowd did not die. Heads leaned together and chins wagged. Throughout the great throng one question was being asked.

What had happened?

No one had tackled Doyce. He had been alone when he fell. He had simply folded up like a jack-knife and slipped to the ground.

What *had* happened?

II

George Allison 'Phones the Yard

HIGH IN C BLOCK, IN THE STADIUM'S EAST STAND, SAT TWO girls who were a study in contrasts. One, blonde, fresh-looking, with an obvious *flair* for clothes and a symmetry of feature more usually associated with faces on chocolate boxes, pursed cyclamen lips and stared across the field of play with frowning grey eyes.

"I wonder—" she began, hesitated, then tried again, "I'm afraid something's—"

She stopped, aware that her companion was regarding her levelly. She turned to meet the gaze of the warm brown eyes. Jill Howard might have been considered good-looking had she not been a foil for her friend, Pat Laruce. She had medium-coloured brown hair that shone with lights and tints of its own, a generous mouth, a clear complexion, and a good figure.

"What's the matter, Pat?"

There was a faint, almost imperceptible challenge to the query.

"Nothing, Jill. I was just wondering what—what had happened?"

"You seem more interested in Jack Doyce than in your fiancé."

Again the challenge sounded, not quite so subdued. The blonde girl lifted her chin. Her eyes narrowed as they surveyed the field. When she spoke her voice was controlled.

"Don't imagine things, Jill. It's just—well, he was injured. That's all. Phil's down there playing strongly."

The brown eyes turned to Phil Morring, playing a sound rear-guard action against Cliff Bastin.

"Phil's wonderful to-day." It was honest acclaim. "He's holding up the Arsenal attack."

The cyclamen lips twitched mockingly.

"You were always the perfect little hero-worshipper, Jill."

A warm flush crept into the other girl's cheeks, and a new bright-ness kindled in her eyes. The hand lying in her lap moved nervously.

"Will you tell me something, Pat?"

"Depends, darling."

"It's just—something…"

"Very well."

"Why aren't you wearing your engagement ring?"

The blonde girl's lips compressed. She watched the game steadily for a few moments before saying, "Oh, I just put it down somewhere and forgot to put it on again. Why"—with an edge of mockery—"does its absence worry you?"

Jill affected a tiny laugh.

"Of course not, silly. I just… wondered."

"Well, don't," came the ready advice. "And don't ask pointless questions—if you don't like getting pointless answers."

If it was a snub it was cleverly delivered. The slurred tone, the quick smile, robbed the words of sting, but did not disturb their meaning.

"Oh—good!"

The blonde girl was clapping her hands, joining in the applause showered on Chulley, the Trojan captain, who had broken up a determined raid by the Arsenal inside forwards.

"Corner!" yelled a spectator behind the girls, as the ball went over the line. The referee glanced at the linesman, and gave a goal kick.

"Open your eyes, ref!" cried the same voice.

Pat Laruce fumbled with the clasp of her handbag, took out a cigarette-case.

"Smoke?" she asked Jill.

"Not just now, thanks. I find the game still interesting—without Doyce."

"Meaning, darling?"

"Why, what should I mean, Pat?"

Jill's surprise was cleverly simulated. The blonde girl chose a cigarette from her case, lit it, and snapped shut her handbag, but not before her companion had caught the gleam of a diamond ring in the bottom of the bag.

"I was never good at mind-reading, dear."

"I didn't misjudge you to that extent, Pat. Oh, look at Phil now!"

Again the Trojan right back served his side valiantly, and the crowd roared its appreciation. But there were now long intervals between the shouts. With the removal of Doyce from the field a change had come over the game, a change that, in some intangible way, seemed to affect both teams alike.

It was as though with Arsenal storming the ramparts of a Troy defended by only ten men the game lost balance. The spectators in the massed stands could not have described how, but they were conscious that the razor keenness of the Trojan attack was blunted. Troy fought, but defensively. Slowly Arsenal became the dictators of the play.

In the Press box, to the left of the Directors' seats, a couple of sports writers lamented Troy's half-back weakness.

"Pity they had to lose that man," said one. "Their forwards can't seem to get going now. They've got to go back for the ball every time. They aren't being fed as they should be."

The other smoked his cigarette and ruminated.

"Bit of bad luck. Unforeseen and damned unfortunate. These Trojans are a fighting side. They're lacking the extra speed Doyce gave the right wing. They're too—lopsided."

The first man grunted, and returned to his notes. "Don't know if Doyce was under the doctor, do you?"

The other man shook his head.

"Kindilett wouldn't have played him had that been the case. The old boy's got too much respect for the game." He glanced at his watch. "Doyce has been off eleven minutes. Must have sprained himself some way. Hallo, Allison's leaving his seat."

They looked towards the Directors' stand. George Allison had risen from his seat at the end of the top row, and was about to pass through the exit.

As a matter of fact, George Allison was wondering what had kept Francis Kindilett from returning to his seat. He wanted to know. The collapse of Doyce was strange, and the Arsenal manager, who in his time had witnessed hundreds of football accidents, had never seen one quite like this. He had an uneasy feeling that everything was not as it appeared on the surface. He couldn't explain the feeling or justify it. It was just a "football hunch." And Kindilett's continued absence did nothing to ease his mind.

He walked down the wide staircase to the entrance hall, where the bronze head of Herbert Chapman regarded all comers with an inscrutable expression, and turned right through a swing-door marked "Private." A sign along the stone corridor read "Visitors' Dressing-room." He turned the handle and entered.

John Doyce lay on a heap of towels, and his naked body gleamed with sweat. Over him stood Francis Kindilett and Tom Whittaker, the Arsenal trainer. Raille, the Trojan trainer, was applying artificial respiration.

"What is it, Francis?"

"God knows, George!" Kindilett's voice was threaded with anxiety. "We can't make it out—none of us. He just doesn't respond."

"Here, let me have a turn."

Whittaker stepped forward and took Raille's place. The Trojan trainer picked up a towel and mopped his streaming face. He said nothing, but he was frowning, as though perplexed.

"What about his heart?" asked Allison.

"He was given a clean bill by the doctor, when we signed him up. That was less than a fortnight ago, so it can't be anything—"

He stopped, aware that the implication was full of dangerous suggestion.

"Better get him into the treatment room, Tom," said Allison to Whittaker.

The two trainers carried the prone player into the treatment room, farther along the corridor, and Raille closed the doors.

"All right, Whittaker, I'll have another go."

Allison turned to Kindilett. "We can't do any good here, Francis. We might as well see the end of the game. They'll probably pull him round and have him on the field in time to boot another goal."

But despite his light words the Arsenal manager experienced no feeling of assurance as he and Kindilett made their way back to the stand and resumed their seats. There was some mystery surrounding Doyce's collapse. The man was in a state of coma, breathing hard, perspiring.

"Is he hurt badly?" asked Mrs Allison as her husband glanced the length of the field, picking up the threads of the play.

"I don't know. I'm puzzled."

A roar from the crowd attracted their attention. Bastin had the ball, and was streaking down the wing. Bryn Jones came across to co-operate. A short, accurate pass from Bastin's racing feet sent the dark-haired Welshman ahead, making for the centre of the field.

The crowd was on its feet now. The unexpected had happened.

Bryn Jones swerved, twisted cleverly round Chulley, and sold a perfect dummy to Crieff. He shot low and hard, and the ball was in the corner of the net.

"Goal!"

"Up the Gunners!"

That goal lifted the crowd's excitement to a higher level. The clapping continued as the teams lined up afresh.

The two reporters who had been interested in Allison's earlier departure lit fresh cigarettes.

"And that's the end," said one, a conclusion the other endorsed by nodding his head. "The game, as a game, is finished."

"All over," the other man agreed, folding his notes. "Crayston and Leslie Jones and Joy won't let them smell the ball any more. How long before time?"

"Six minutes."

Farther along in the East Stand Pat Laruce and Jill Howard were settling a point of play.

"Phil would never have been tricked as Crieff was," the latter contended, watching Morring effect a good clearance.

"I don't know," said the blonde girl. "I think Bastin wouldn't have started the movement if John Doyce had been out there."

Little lines appeared at the sides of her mouth as her lips pursed. "I wonder what happened, Jill. He should be out again."

"He should if he wants his team to win—or even draw now. Oh, good!" Jill suddenly exclaimed as Morring robbed Drake of the ball and took it up the centre himself, to send it accurately to Wellock, lying back, waiting for it. "Don't you feel proud of him, Pat?" she said excitedly, turning to the other girl.

But the blonde girl could not have heard. She was staring across the field with a fixity of gaze that told the other girl she saw nothing of the play.

"Why, Pat—what's wrong?"

Pat Laruce started. "Nothing, Jill—nothing. I was just thinking. That's all. I—I—Oh, it's nothing, I tell you," she broke off, a note of irritation in her tone.

Three minutes before the end of the game Allison left his seat and was joined by Kindilett, whose face was glum.

"I suppose I was hoping for the impossible, George," he said, with a faint smile. "And I should have known the impossible never happens."

"Your boys played marvellously," Allison assured him. "They've got stamina, they know how to shoot, they're clean, their movements are crisp, and their positioning is—"

"But they didn't win, George."

Allison glanced at his companion. He had known Francis Kindilett over a number of years, and entertained considerable respect for his insight and abilities as a builder of amateur football teams. Years before there had been the Saxon Rovers. Then tragedy had touched his life, and he had tried to replant his roots afresh. It had been a hard job. No one save Kindilett himself knew how hard. Allison could only guess. But the man had doggedly set to work to build up Britain's amateur soccer. He had won through. There had been obstacles, many and varied. They had been overcome, and he must have entertained hopes—eventual hopes...

"No, Francis, they didn't win, but it was a close thing, and if Doyce hadn't gone down—" Allison shrugged. "From the way the second half opened, anything could have happened."

Kindilett gave him a straight look.

"Something did."

They said no more. In the treatment room the two trainers were still working over the unresponsive right half.

"It's got me beat," Whittaker admitted. "There's no bruise on him, not a mark. He wasn't injured on the field. It's—uncanny."

Allison glanced at Raille.

"You think the same, Raille?"

Raille was staring at Kindilett. His glance left the Trojan manager's face reluctantly.

"You'll have to get a doctor, Mr Kindilett. It isn't something... ordinary."

Kindilett caught his breath.

"You mean, Raille?"

The trainer's face was stiff. "I don't know what I mean," he said. "He doesn't respond to anything."

They stood there for a moment, each occupied with his own thoughts, until a clatter of running feet in the corridor and a bang on the door announced that the game was over and the players were returning to the dressing-rooms. Allison opened the door. Outside stood Chulley, the Trojan captain, his shirt and knickers attesting to the hard struggle he had put up in his team's defence.

"How is Doyce?" he asked.

A head and a half taller than the Arsenal manager, he stood staring at the towel-draped figure on the treatment table.

"Not so good. Better leave things now, Chulley," said Kindilett.

"Sure." Chulley's voice was uncertain. "But if there's anything I can do—I mean—"

"Thanks, Chulley. I'll remember. Er—there wasn't another goal in the last minute?"

"No."

The Trojan captain turned away, trying to hide his disappointment at the result. Allison closed the door and came back to Kindilett.

"Francis," he said gravely, "I think I ought to mention it, in case the worst happens, but—"

"You mean Doyce dies?"

Allison nodded. "Yes, that's what I mean."

"You think that's the worst that can happen?"

Whittaker stooped over the body on the table. Raille frowned at Doyce's tousled head.

"I don't understand, Francis," said Allison, looking hard at the Trojan manager.

Kindlilett waved a hand. "Never mind, George. It was just—a thought. I—" He broke off, staring at Whittaker, who was bending very close over Doyce, holding the player's face. "What is it? What have you found? Is—"

Whittaker's dark blue pullover straightened. His face, red, gleaming with moisture, turned to the speaker.

"I'm afraid it's all over, Mr Kindilett," he announced, drawing the towel over Doyce's head.

"Good God! Are you sure?" said Allison quickly, moving forward.

Whittaker nodded, looked at Raille, who stood as though dazed.

"He never came properly round."

The two team managers stared at the towel-shrouded figure, then at each other.

"There will be an inquest, and a lot of publicity," murmured Allison. "I think I know now, Francis, what you meant when you said—"

The Arsenal manager paused, conscious that the two trainers were staring fixedly at him. He had to make a decision, and it was hard.

"Francis," he said, "we've got to face facts. Doyce is dead. The circumstances of his death are peculiar, to say the least. I'm afraid I'll have to get in touch with the police."

The words fell like pebbles into the quiet of a well. Kindilett stiffened. A look of anguish crossed his face.

"Then, George"—there was an awed hush to his tones—"you think something—that—"

He couldn't put his thought into words. It was too fantastic, too incredible.

"I think you'd better stay here in case some of the Press boys come along for a statement, Francis. Put them off. I'm going up to my office, and put through a call to the Yard. This is something for them to take care of."

For a moment Kindilett stood staring into space, as though he had not heard. He pulled himself together suddenly.

"Very well, George," he murmured. "If that's what you think is best."

Allison gave him a quick glance, and went out, making no further comment. Three minutes later the receiver against his ear clicked as a connexion was made and a clear voice said, "Scotland Yard."

III

Inspector Slade Arrives

THE DISPERSAL OF SEVENTY THOUSAND SPECTATORS IS NOT achieved in a few minutes. At the top of Highbury Hill foot and mounted police controlled the queues invading the Arsenal Station of the Underground. More mounted police kept the crowd in Avenell Road on the move. All the tributary roads were choked with cars that had been parked throughout the game. A score of taxi-drivers who had seen an opportunity of combining business with pleasure that afternoon now tried to worm their cabs through the throng, which took singularly small notice of honking horns and verbal exasperation. Peanut vendors and newsboys were exercising their lungs and taking a steady flow of coppers for their trouble. Over the crowd hung a pall of tobacco smoke and dust.

"Come on now. Move along there."

The good-humoured invitations of the police produced little apparent result. There is something viscous and sluggish about the mass movements of a football crowd that is homeward bound. Having witnessed a game, it seemingly has only one thought, to know the results of games played in every other corner of the Kingdom.

"Chelsea again—"

"See the Wolves got a netful."

"What did the Wednesday do?"

"Another away win for Everton…"

"Got the Scottish results in your paper? How about the Rangers and Aberdeen?"

Pencils check the first batch of published results with pool forecasts. Anxious inquiries are answered with almost savage terseness.

"Draw… won away… lost at home…"

Slowly the bright possibility of those other match results fades, and interest returns to the game that has been watched. Fresh cigarettes are lit, more peanuts and chewing-gum are bought and munched, and discussion begins, sometimes heated, sometimes very partisan and not sincere, but never disinterested.

And all the time that shuffling, mooching crowd that has overflowed on to every inch of pavement, gutter, and roadway is slowly pouring into Underground trains, buses, cars, and motor-coaches. There is plenty of shoving with elbows, trampling of less nimble feet, and poking of more prominent ribs. In the trains the corridors and entrance platforms are choked. Cigarettes are knocked from mouths and clothes are singed. Hands press heavily on strangers' shoulders.

"Sorry, mate."

"That's all right, old man. We all got to get home, ain't we?"

The air is full of expunged breath, smoke, human smells, and heat. But there is plenty of laughter, plenty of Cockney chaff. Whatever happens, however great the discomfort, the crowd keeps its good-temper. This herded homegoing is just part of the afternoon's entertainment. The bigger the crowd the bigger the crush, and correspondingly the bigger the individual's satisfaction at being there.

"Record gate to-day, eh?"

"Must be."

"Glad I didn't miss it."

"Me too."

That rib-bruising, foot-crushing scramble is endured with something of pride. It is the final proof that the individual has not been wasting his time, that the game was worth seeing because everybody else wanted to see it. A generalization that holds strangely true throughout the entire soccer season.

Of course, there are the few who protest at the crush. But the real followers of football, the "regulars," the "supporters," who make the Leagues possible and provide Britain with a professional sport in which she is supreme, they have only a tight-lipped contempt for these casual spectators—and occasionally a helpful suggestion.

But like every other natural tide, the football crowd leaves behind it tiny pools, groups who persist in debating some point of play on a street-corner, and of course at Highbury there is always that bigger pool that remains doggedly at the Stadium entrance.

These are the hundred per cent. fans, the autograph-hunters, and the admirers of individual players. An hour, two hours after a game is over some of them are still there, unwearied, constant of mind and purpose.

These are the core of the soccer crowd, professional spectators, as it were. They follow "their" team as a gull follows a ship, unswervingly, persistently. In the large window of present-day social entertainment they find a place with the professional first-nighters of the theatre and the professional clubmen of the West End, those Mayfair troglodytes who emerge into the open once every twenty-four hours, to see if the world still wags—outside the columns of *The Times*.

But while the crowd of seventy thousand take more than an hour to disperse a much more animated scene occurs in the dressing-rooms where the players relax.

Few of the Arsenal players, after that memorable match with the Trojans, noticed the worried look on Tom Whittaker's face when he joined them. As Whittaker took the cup of tea some one pushed into his hands, Eddie Hapgood was delivering himself as a veteran.

"They were as good as any First Division side we've met this season," he averred.

Swindin, warming his bare feet on the heated green tiling of the floor, nodded. "That Doyce has got a kick. I didn't sniff the ball when he took that penalty."

"Bredge was a clever schemer," called Bernard Joy, pulling his fair, tousled head clear of a muddied shirt. "He held that front line together."

"Wonder what happened to Doyce," put in George Male, crooking an arm round a knee. "He went down like a ninepin."

"Anyone want another cup of tea?" called Drake, at the table by the door. He stood statuesque, teapot held over his craning dark head.

"Hey, Ted," said Kirchen, "you were near Doyce. What bowled him over?"

"Haven't an idea. Far as I could see nobody touched him. Tom"—Drake's soft Hampshire voice lifted as he addressed the Arsenal trainer—"know what happened to their right half?"

Whittaker appeared to take no notice. He spoke to Bastin, pouring some embrocation on his hands. He rubbed the Arsenal outside left's ankle until it shone redly.

"Tom!" called the persistent centre-forward.

"Hullo." Whittaker glanced round, but continued the massaging operation.

"What happened to Doyce? Heard anything?"

"He's still in the treatment room, I understand," the trainer stalled.

Players darted into the spacious bathroom. In the large bath heads bobbed like corks into a rolling cloud of steam. Hapgood dived for the soap, finally got it from Jack Crayston, and a free-for-all tussle started. Suddy water rose in a cascade, hit the flooring with a dull smack.

"Hey!" called Male. "Take it easy! You're—"

His complaint ended as a violent splutter when Hapgood jumped on his shoulders.

"Whoa, horse! Whoa!" cried the irrepressible Arsenal captain.

Male's response was to dump the temporary equestrian on his back and fling a bar of yellow soap at his head.

The room rang with high-spirited shouts. Under a stinging cold shower Kirchen danced round in a high-stepping circle. Suddenly darting from the shower, and snatching up an enormous towel that enfolded his body like a bud in a leaf, he ran into the dressing-room. Behind him padded the others, dripping water, shaking their dank heads, smacking one another's backs with no pretended heartiness.

They shrieked and yodelled and towelled their bodies until they glowed. Tom Whittaker, face red and moist, walked among them, pausing to flick an ear or deliver a friendly jab in the ribs as they scrambled into their everyday clothes again.

There was plenty of routine, after-the-match work for the Arsenal trainer. Swindin's arm had to be massaged again. The sharp tang of the rubbing liquid quickly filled the room. The sleeves of his shirt rolled up, Whittaker tended his charges with the care that is given only to footballers, boxers, and babies.

Deft, experienced fingers worked on bruises, rubbing out their soreness and discoloration.

The noise and horseplay stopped. Whittaker looked up. George Allison stood in the room, looking over the half-dressed group.

Eyes of trainer and manager met in one quick, understanding glance.

"You did well, boys," said George Allison, slipping a hand into a trousers pocket. "They've said some hard things about you this season, but the stuff you did out there this afternoon was the answer."

The players continued with their dressing. There was something else to come. They sensed it.

"However, I haven't come to pat you on the back," said the Arsenal manager. "Something serious has happened." The loose change in his pocket jingled. He had been fingering his monocle. The black cord now slipped through his fingers. "Doyce, their right half," he said gravely, "is dead."

The players stared at one another and at Allison. Ted Drake shot a glance at Whittaker, but the trainer's eyes were lowered in a frown. One of the men dropped a shoe. Its clatter was unnoticed.

Then they were all speaking at once, questioning Allison and gathering round him.

"All I can tell you," he said, "is that I have told Scotland Yard, and Inspector Slade is on his way here. He'll have questions to ask you, and I want you to tell him anything you can. This thing may be more serious than anyone of us realizes. None of you must leave until he has seen you."

The commissionaire entered the room, and gave Allison a bundle of paper tape, the results of the afternoon's League matches. Usually the Arsenal players were keen to know how other teams had fared. But their interest was gone. They listened to Allison reading the results, but their minds were elsewhere.

"Well," said the manager, finishing the list of the day's results, "I guess that's all for now. But don't forget. None of you leaves until Inspector Slade's given you the O.K."

Crayston turned to Bernard Joy.

"Dead. It doesn't seem possible," he muttered.

"I suppose, Jack," said the schoolmaster, "you're thinking he—" He paused. "He was a right half, too."

Crayston ran a comb through his curly hair.

"Yes, Bernard, and I suppose you're thinking he was an amateur, like yourself."

Joy knotted his "lucky" tie.

"I don't like the sound of it," he said. "Tom knows something and won't tell us. See how he's been acting since he came in? Now look at his face."

Whittaker had finished with the players, and was peeling off his clothes, preparing to take a stinging shower. Tom was more worried than he would have admitted. He towelled himself and dressed quietly. He was going over in his mind the play he had seen from the trainers' glass-enclosed stand. He knew none of the Arsenal players was responsible for Doyce's falling to the ground so mysteriously.

But that would not prevent a great deal of ugly publicity. He knew that too. There would be rumours and talk, and Arsenal would find themselves in a publicity glare stronger than they had ever received from the usual business of transfers. Tom Whittaker was an Arsenal man seven days a week, and he was worried because he could not see how Arsenal were going to come out of this. It was going to be unpleasant having Yard detectives taking a close interest in his personal routine.

The door opened again, and the commissionaire reappeared. "Inspector Slade, sir," he said to George Allison, and added unnecessarily, "from Scotland Yard."

Allison met Slade in the entrance hall. The Yard man had two companions.

"Mr Allison?" he asked, holding out his hand. "This is Dr Meadows and my assistant, Sergeant Clinton." Allison nodded, shook hands, and looked from the grey-haired medico to the bullet-headed, dour-featured sergeant, and then to Slade, grey-eyed, with a square fighter's jaw and an athlete's body. There was something about the detective that told Allison no time would be wasted with the police investigation. Here was a man of action, who could make up his mind quickly and readily come to a decision with himself.

"The body is in the treatment room," he told Slade.

"In that case," Slade decided, "Dr Meadows had better make his examination now. I'll join you later, doctor. If you'll show the doctor, Mr Allison—"

"Of course. This way, Dr Meadows."

In a minute the Arsenal manager had returned.

"Perhaps you would like to come up to my office, Inspector," he invited. "The teams are finishing dressing, and meantime I've got the manager of the Trojans in my room."

Slade nodded. Allison led the way. Francis Kindilett rose from a chair when the newcomers entered. Allison introduced them. Slade, watching the other man closely, saw that he was nervous and very distressed.

"Perhaps you would prefer to tell me, in your own words, just what happened," he suggested.

Kindilett, who had been dreading the arrival of a Scotland Yard man, flashed him a grateful glance. Haltingly he told the little there was to tell. Slade listened attentively. Clinton, in the background, made some notes in a notebook.

When Kindilett stopped Slade said, "Doyce had a football reputation, then, Mr Kindilett?"

"Yes. He has been very well known in amateur football for some years," said Kindilett. "Mr Allison here will agree." Allison nodded. "One or two League clubs have been after him."

"Common knowledge in soccer circles," Allison added. "But he's always been a bit independent, hasn't he, Francis?"

"Yes, that's so. Actually he's a business partner of another Trojan player—Philip Morring, our right back."

"I see. Did Morring have anything to do with Doyce joining your club?" asked Slade.

"No, nothing," said Kindilett readily. "As a matter of fact, they are insurance brokers, and both of them played in public-school football."

"You've known Doyce some while?"

Kindilett hesitated. "I knew him some years ago, but I'd lost touch with him until he signed with us some ten days or so ago. Setchley, our outside right, brought him to the notice of the committee."

"Then this was his first match with the Trojans?"

"Yes."

There was a tap on the door. Raille entered. Kindilett introduced him.

"This is our trainer, George Raille, Inspector. I think he might be able to tell you more about the package that came for Doyce during the match."

"Package?"

"Yes," Raille explained. "It came by District Messenger about quarter-past three. We came back into the dressing-room at half-time—that was about half-past three—and the commissionaire handed it over to me."

"You gave it to Doyce?"

"Yes."

"He opened it?"

"Yes, I saw him do that. But I haven't any idea what was in it. I seem to remember him crossing to his clothes, though."

"Where are his clothes?"

Raille glanced at Allison, who explained. "They're in the treatment room, Inspector, with the body. I had them put there so that no one should tamper with them. Then I locked the doors. I unlocked them for Dr Meadows just a few minutes ago."

"Very good, Mr Allison," said the Yard man. He turned back to Raille. "Anything else you can tell me about Doyce? Did he get on well with the other players?"

"So far as I can tell," said the trainer. "Though, come to think of it, he and Morring rather steered clear of each other, if I can put it that way."

"You can put it any way you like, Raille," said Slade meaningly, "so long as you're telling me something and that something's the truth. So there was some feeling between Doyce and Morring. That what you mean?"

"I don't think I'd go so far as to say that," Raille hedged.

Slade glanced across at Kindilett. The man looked more worried now.

"All right," said the Yard detective, "I'll see what Morring has to say himself. Meantime I'll have a look at the body, if Dr Meadows is through."

The treatment room at the Arsenal Stadium lies between the home team's dressing-room and the dressing-room reserved for visiting teams. Between it and the visitors' room is a small office reserved for Whittaker. This office has a door opening out into the main corridor and another door leading into the treatment room, which in turn has a door on the far side leading into the Arsenal dressing-room.

Locking both treatment room doors, therefore, had effectively sealed the room.

Slade walked in, to find the police surgeon rolling down his shirt-sleeves. Clinton followed him in and closed the door.

"Well, doctor?"

Dr Meadows looked up. "Ah, Inspector, a very interesting case—very. The *post-mortem* should certainly prove poisoning. Organic poisoning of some kind. He perspired very freely, the pupils of his eyes are dilated. Yet there is no mark on the tongue or teeth, and no odour. Looks like a subcutaneous injection. That would mean a skin puncture. And that"—the doctor slipped into his jacket—"is as far as I can go. The poison might be anything from—well"—his mouth pursed—"curare, which would be very unusual, to, say, atropine, which is an alkaloid derivative."

"And just what does that make the case?" Slade asked bluntly.

The police surgeon fingered his chin thoughtfully.

"It could be suicide, though I doubt it—doubt it very much," he added. "Why should any man kill himself in these surroundings? The idea's fantastic. No, far more likely to be murder."

Slade caught the glance levelled at him by Clinton. They moved towards the table covered by a large towel. Carefully the two men searched the dead footballer's body for some tell-tale sign that would uphold what Dr Meadows had said.

They were still searching when the doctor picked up his bag and said, "Well, I'll be getting along, Slade. I'll let you have the report as soon as I can."

"Thanks, doctor."

The door closed after the police surgeon.

Clinton straightened his back. "So we now have a football murder on our hands. This is going to be a sweet job. Scores of players to question, none of 'em remembering a damned thing."

He made no attempt to conceal his disgust. Slade looked up, smiled grimly. He and Clinton had worked together for years, on a number of cases. Each entertained a very great respect for the other's capacities.

"What's troubling you, Clinton?"

The sergeant drew the towel up over the dead man's legs.

"I've got a feeling that whoever pulled this job planned things so as to have no slip-up. What a time to kill a man—in the middle of a match!"

"Not very sporting," said Slade dryly.

"Sporting!" grunted the sergeant. "I bet this bird never knew what was happening to him, though he looks the kind that might have asked for trouble. Dark hair, bit effeminate in features, well built. But mouth too thin, eyes a bit too close together—"

"Look, Clinton!"

The sergeant's remarks were cut short by his superior's exclamation. He moved to Slade's side. The Inspector was holding the dead man's left hand, examining the fleshy part of the thumb.

He pointed to a tiny blood clot, which looked, at first glance, like a speck of dried mud.

"What do you make of that?"

Clinton bent close. "Certainly might be a prick such as Dr Meadows referred to," he agreed. "But how the devil—"

He glanced questioningly at Slade.

"There was that package, which arrived before half-time," Slade reminded Clinton. "I don't think we shall have to look much farther than that. Here, I see, is the wrapping paper. Evidently Allison or some one thought to put it in here with the clothes."

From another table he picked up a sheet of brown wrapping paper. Doyce's name and the address of the Arsenal Club were printed in inked capitals, clearly and neatly. With the paper was a cardboard box and a small square envelope. The envelope had a tiny hole in the middle of one side, as though something sharp, like a pin, had pierced it. The cardboard box was unmarked.

"This is interesting." Slade pointed out the pricked hole in the envelope. "Make anything of it, Clinton?"

The sergeant nodded.

"Looks as though it might correspond with that prick on Doyce's thumb."

"True, Clinton, but there's something else," Slade remarked. "The left hand is the hand with which a right-handed person would hold an envelope while tearing open the flap with the right hand."

"That's so," Clinton agreed. "Then there must have been something fairly flat and with a sharp point in the envelope, like a—"

"Drawing-pin?"

"Yes, that would fit it. He holds the envelope tight in the left hand and the pin pricks his thumb. The pin is poisoned, and the murder's finished. Simple as that."

"Yes. I'm afraid finding the real answer isn't going to be quite so simple, Clinton. Let's have a look through his clothes before we do anything else."

They found the customary pen and wallet and loose change, a bunch of keys, a handkerchief, some folded bus tickets, and in one pocket a Press cutting.

The cutting read:

> "A farm worker saw the blonde curls floating on the water. The body was taken from East Gate Fosse. She had been dead some hours. The jury returned a verdict of Death by Misadventure."

The cutting was made up of separate sentences taken out of their context and pasted together.

"This may mean much or nothing," said Slade, pocketing the cutting. "Meantime, Clinton, you'd better start collecting together all the pins you can find."

"Pins?" queried the sergeant.

"Tie-pins. I noticed Allison wore an unusual one. And there's a notice-board outside this room. It's studded with drawing-pins. Take the lot—and handle them carefully." Slade drew the towel over the dead man's face. "Then let Irvin come in and get to work finger-printing this room, and we'll have half a dozen shots taken of the room. I'm going to see the teams now. We can't keep them any longer."

I V

Morring Makes a Request

I N THE CORRIDOR OUTSIDE THE TREATMENT ROOM SLADE FOUND Allison and Kindilett smoking. Both managers looked at him inquiringly as he appeared.

"Well, Inspector?" asked the Arsenal manager.

"I'm afraid Dr Meadows doesn't think it was an accident," said the Yard detective.

Allison looked grave. Kindilett's mouth sagged noticeably at the corners.

"There's one thing I think you should know, Inspector," said Allison. "When this match was planned I arranged with Mr Kindilett for the Trojan team to remain in London as guests of the Arsenal Club. As I saw it, they could then put in a spot of training here, at the Stadium. To-morrow has already been fixed for a round of golf at the Dyke course, near Brighton, where the Arsenal team often spend some time training during the season. I thought I'd mention this, before you speak to the boys, because in this case you may prefer to question some of them later, now you know they'll be together."

"Thank you, Mr Allison," said the detective. "That does rather simplify things." He turned to Kindilett. "The Trojans, I understand, are players in different social classes."

"That's so," nodded their manager. "Torburn, our goalie, is a carpenter. He lives the other side of St Albans. Morring, on the other hand, as I believe I've already mentioned, is an insurance broker. The team has one thing in common—a desire to play good football. I've been four years building up the Trojans. But"—a note of pride crept into his low voice—"it's been worth it."

"I doubt, Francis," put in Allison, "if any other man in England could have done the job."

Slade realized that the words were meant. They were an honest tribute to the man who had built the Trojan team.

He stood back, and Allison opened the door of the Arsenal dressing-room. The floor had been swabbed down. Shirts and knickers and socks and boots had been collected and removed. The large white bath-towels with the embroidered red "Arsenal" in one corner had been taken away to the laundry in charge of veteran Punch McEwan. Arsenal and Trojan players stood conversing in low tones. The air was now cleared of steam and the tang of rubbing fluids, but faintly blue with the smoke from half a dozen cigarettes.

"Inspector Slade," Allison announced, "has some questions to ask you."

He stood back, and the Yard man moved forward.

"Mr Kindilett has described what happened on the field," he said. "I understand Doyce scored a penalty goal. That meant you kicked off again for the Arsenal, Drake," he added, turning to the well-known centre-forward.

Ted Drake folded his arms and frowned.

"Yes, that's right," he agreed. "I passed to Bryn."

"And I put it over to Gordon," said Bryn Jones.

Gordon Bremner nodded.

"I remember," put in Whittaker, "the follow-through was a wing movement. The ball came right across from Kirchen to Bryn Jones, and Doyce was quite close to Bryn. He was anticipating very well."

Slade turned to the Welshman. "Do you remember what happened next?"

Bryn Jones's face wrinkled thoughtfully.

"Yes," he said, "Tom's right. I remember now. Doyce was coming in pretty fast—"

"Did you look at him?"

Bryn Jones glanced up, surprised. "Well, no, I can't say I did—not to look at him closely, I mean."

"That's what I meant," nodded Slade. "You didn't note, for instance, how he seemed to shape?"

"No."

"But you would have noticed anything unusual about him, I take it? Had he been breathing hard, sweating profusely—anything like that?"

"I think I can help you there," put in Cliff Bastin.

Slade turned to the speaker.

"You noticed something?"

"Yes," said the outside left. "Bryn swung the ball to me when Doyce came across—"

"I remember," nodded Whittaker. "Anticipating the movement, Doyce continued straight on to the wing. He tackled you, didn't he, Cliff?"

Bastin ran a hand across his straight blond hair, and hunched his shoulders a little.

"Yes, Doyce came at me pretty fast, but I just had time to put the ball back."

"I'll say you did," put in Leslie Jones. "Nearly over the line."

"But what did you notice about Doyce?" Slade asked Bastin.

"His breath was coming fast, though that wasn't anything unusual. But I did notice he was sweating freely. His hair was moist and tangled up, too. I wondered at the time if he was really in condition."

"He was as fit as a carthorse when we ran the rule over him," Raille avowed. "But, Bastin," he added, turning to the Arsenal player, "wasn't that just about when Doyce went down? I saw Leslie Jones dash up, save the ball from going off the island, and boot it well up to a forward. I think it was Drake. Anyway, Crieff got the ball, kicked it, and then every one was shouting."

There were some moments while players sorted out their impressions. But Raille's words apparently summarized the last piece of play before Doyce's collapse.

Slade nodded to Bastin. "Then you were the last player to be tackled by Doyce?"

"Yes, I suppose so," Bastin agreed.

The Yard man asked a number of further questions, and the assembly tried its best to provide answers that added to the sum total of the detective's knowledge. But Slade made little further headway, for the simple reason that there was none to be made.

Doyce's collapse had been as mysterious as it had been sudden. Not a player on the field at the time could offer any information that would begin to clear up the mystery.

Slade turned back to Allison.

"Well," he said, "I think that winds up what I can do with them just now. There's just one point I'd like you to explain if you would—"

"Anything I can, Inspector."

"Sergeant Clinton is gathering up all sharp-pointed obstacles, tie-pins, drawing-pins—yes, we're going to take precautions. There's a chance that Doyce met his death by a prick of some sort. We don't want a repetition."

Allison's face revealed his amazement.

"Good God, Inspector! Then that means Doyce was—"

"We'd better wait for the *post-mortem* examination before we make up our minds," said Slade quietly.

Allison nodded. "I'll have a word with the boys before they leave. Er"—he fingered his own tie-pin—"does that mean Sergeant Clinton will want this?"

Slade smiled faintly. "If I know Clinton, he will."

Allison grinned. "I see. Very well, Inspector. Ah, here is the sergeant."

Slade turned, to find Clinton behind him. A glance at the sergeant's face revealed that he had something he wanted to tell his superior. Slade drew him aside.

"What is it, Clinton?"

"We haven't got much from the finger-printing," the sergeant announced. "Irvin's been all over the place, but there's not a clear set in the room. Every one's smeared. It struck me we might get some shots of how Doyce fell on the ground before the crowd here goes."

Slade nodded.

"That's an idea. I'll have a word with the trainers."

Whittaker and Raille agreed to go on the field with several players and reconstruct the play just before Doyce fell, marking the various positions. The players, the two trainers, and the sergeant went off. Slade approached Kindilett.

"I'd like to have a word upstairs with Morring," said the Yard man. "And who did you say was responsible for Doyce's joining the team?"

"Setchley, our outside right. That's him over there, with Hapgood—the man with the darkish-red hair."

Slade looked in the direction in which the Trojan manager indicated, and saw a slim man of medium height and rather surprisingly pale face crowned with dark auburn hair.

"Has he any connexion with the Morring-Doyce insurance business?" asked the detective.

"No," said Kindilett. "Setchley is, in some respects, the strangest of my bunch."

"In what way?"

"As a footballer. By profession he's a research chemist."

With difficulty Slade repressed a start of surprise. But he was aware that Kindilett was watching him with cold eyes.

"That's very interesting," he said.

"Why?" demanded the Trojan manager.

There was a trace of something hostile about Kindilett's manner. Slade marked it, and was puzzled to account for it.

"Oh, just that he may be able to help me with a few details," he said smoothly. "The analytical mind, you know."

Kindilett nodded abruptly, and turned away. Slade stood looking after him. The Yard man was convinced from what he had seen and heard that Doyce's death had been premeditated, that it had been very carefully arranged, and that he had died from some form of poisoning. So far as his preliminary examination allowed him to give any opinion at all, that was what Dr Meadows had confirmed. And Meadows, as Slade knew, was a knowing bird. He had been writing reports on police cases long enough to know a murder when he saw it.

His suggestion in the present case was that Doyce had been murdered by a subcutaneous injection of one of the less common, but more potent, alkaloid poisons.

Now, on top of this, Kindilett had gratuitously offered the information that a member of the Trojan team was a research chemist, a man who could procure, quite readily, such a deadly poison.

And the man who presumably was something of a poison expert was the member of the team who had sponsored the dead man's membership.

Did that add up to anything?

A touch on his arm dragged Slade's thoughts back to his immediate surroundings. A pleasant-faced man of square build was regarding him with a pair of troubled grey eyes.

"Yes?" said Slade.

"My name's Morring, Inspector. I'd rather like to have a word with you."

Slade gave the other a keen look. Here was the man he was anxious to interview coming to meet him more than half-way. However, it was no part of his plan to appear anxious for information from the dead man's partner.

"Very well, if it's important."

"It's important," said Morring.

His tone conveyed the impression that he spoke the truth. Whatever Morring had to tell Slade *was* important—to Philip Morring.

"Very well, let's go upstairs."

Morring followed the Yard man up to Allison's office. Slade closed the door. They had the room to themselves.

"Sit down," he invited.

Morring drew a chair up to the centre of the room. From a ceiling lamp soft light fell on the footballer's dark head. There was a brief silence, broken by the ticking of the grandfather clock trying to outpace the painted wall-clock over the mantelpiece behind the desk. From outside in the street below various noises drifted up—the roar of a car's engine, the cry of a newsboy, a sudden fading laugh.

Slade spoke. "You have something to tell me, I believe?"

The words roused Morring. He sat up, the light shining full on his troubled face.

"Frankly, I don't know how to begin," he said.

Slade, who always tried to put a witness at his ease, relaxed visibly.

"The beginning's as good a place to start as any other," he said lightly. "Often better. Smoke?"

Morring shook his head.

"No, thanks." For a moment a smile touched his strongly chiselled mouth, but when he spoke again it was gone. "Let me say, then, first of all, Inspector, that Doyce and I were in the same school team, and we always got on fairly well. When we left school we had similar ideas about how to make a living. Quite a drop of water has passed under the bridge since those days, but the upshot was we started a joint business."

"In London?" asked Slade, as though this were news.

"Yes, in the City. We opened our own office as insurance brokers. As you may suppose, neither of us was particularly flush with coin. We had the prospect of hard work and small profits. But we weren't deterred. We were both bachelors, and had no ties. However, very early in our business arrangement we came to one definite decision. That was to safeguard the firm."

"How?" probed Slade when the other man hesitated.

"We took out a dual insurance policy. It was, I assure you, only as protection for the firm, in case something happened to one of us. The other would then be able to continue unhampered."

"How much was the amount?" asked Slade.

The blunt question caused the footballer to straighten in his chair.

"Ten thousand pounds," he said.

"I see. A tidy sum." Slade saw Morring's fists clench, but the man kept his feelings in check. "Did any conditions of the policy prevent payment being made in the event of death of one of you by violence?"

Morring's face went bleak. A glaze froze the expression in his eyes.

"No, there was no cancelling murder clause in the policy," he said throatily.

"So that through your partner's death this afternoon you will benefit to the extent of ten thousand pounds?"

Morring got to his feet. He leaned towards Slade over Allison's large desk.

"You think that a good motive, Inspector?" he said bitterly.

"Motive for what?" Slade parried.

Morring breathed hard. He waved a hand, as though to rid himself of something cluttering his mind.

"Oh, don't stall, man!" he said testily. "I know you're not here because John Doyce fell down and broke his neck. You're here because Doyce was murdered, and—and that ten thousand pounds is going to make things look sweet for me. I could see where I was getting. I had to speak to you."

"Sit down, try to relax," suggested Slade to the other.

"Relax!"

"Nevertheless, try. You sound as though you're ready to go off at half-cock—"

"Well, how would you feel, sitting around and knowing Doyce has got what he asked for, and probably—"

"Just a minute," said the Yard man, leaning forward. "So Doyce had been making enemies?"

Morring got himself in hand, sat down.

"He was a great lad with the ladies. Luckily, it didn't injure business. Another thing, we kept our private lives strictly separate. What I did was my business. What he did was his. It worked out very well for the office. We were, in a way, complementary partners. The other supplied what the one lacked."

"But some of his private life overflowed?"

"That's one way of putting it. He was always getting mixed up with some woman or other, and then getting untangled again. I'll give him full credit for being the world's champion wriggler—in that regard."

"You sound as though he might have upset you?"

Morring sat still, trying to control his breathing. When he spoke his temper was still in check.

"Let's not beat about the bush," he said. "Doyce and I kept our distance—socially. It suited us. You'll probably learn that I wasn't keen to have him in the Trojan Club. I wasn't—that's all. But being his partner, I'd sooner tell you all this voluntarily, than leave you to find it out. That understandable?"

"Certainly." Slade, watching the other closely, saw his mouth shut firmly. The detective knew that he would get no more real information without probing deeply. Morring had said his piece. "Would you mind giving me Doyce's address?"

"Flat 17, Belloge Court. It's in Baker Street."

"Thanks. One last question. You don't know of anyone who had threatened your partner?"

A smile touched Morring's thin lips. "A murderous threat? No. But I myself have in the past threatened to black his eye."

"And did you?"

The directness of the question threw the man a little off guard. "Why, no, I—" His glance narrowed. "Sorry, Inspector. I should have been prepared for a sense of humour."

He went out, leaving the Yard man staring at a large griffin, fashioned in silver and horn. A gift to George Allison from the Welsh Football Association. Slade reached for a telephone near his hand.

"Get me Scotland Yard," he requested the operator.

A few seconds later he was talking to the Assistant-Commissioner in charge of the C.I.D. He gave a very brief report of what he had found, and made a request for the Yard to cover the District Messenger lead.

"When I leave here I'm going to the Baker Street flat," Slade added.

He dropped the receiver in its cradle as the door opened, and Allison entered, accompanied by the commissionaire who had announced the detective's arrival.

"I thought you were free, Inspector," said the Arsenal manager, glancing at the 'phone. "I saw Morring just now—"

"I was admiring this griffin," said Slade.

Allison ran his finger over the griffin's head.

"They gave me that to mark an occasion when they had three of my players in a Welsh international team." His hand drew back. "I came to tell you, Inspector, that the commissionaire has reminded me that a young lady called to see Doyce shortly after the match. I had just 'phoned the Yard and come downstairs. She was speaking to him."

Slade turned to the man.

"She wanted to see Doyce?"

"She wanted to know what had happened to him, first. When I said I didn't know she became kind of agitated, and asked if she could see him. Mr Allison came up just then."

"She then asked me the same questions," said Allison, "and I told her Doyce was dead and I had just 'phoned the Yard. Her hand flew to her mouth and she cried, 'Dead!' as though she couldn't believe it. Then without another word she turned and ran out of the building. The incident had slipped my mind till the commissionaire reminded me just now."

Slade digested what he had been told.

"Can you describe the girl?" he asked.

Allison looked at the commissionaire. The man screwed up his face, said, "She was a blonde, pretty too, and she used a light purple lipstick. She wore a light-coloured coat and a hat with a veil. That's all I can say definitely."

"Very well," said the Yard man. "Now while you're here there's one other thing. You were in the entrance hall throughout the first half?" he asked the commissionaire.

"Yes," the man nodded.

"Did you see anyone enter the corridor to the players' wing?"

"Only one or two of the regular staff."

"You're certain?" Slade pressed.

"Absolutely," the man affirmed. "I stood by the swing door the whole time."

"What about after the second half had started? Anyone come through then?"

"Only Punch."

"Punch?"

"Punch McEwan, our laundryman," Allison enlarged. "The laundry is at the far side of the building."

"I see," said Slade slowly. "And there is a way out of the training wing through the laundry?"

"Yes, into the East Stand," said the Arsenal manager. "I know that some of the players who are not in a team on any particular Saturday often borrow the key from McEwan and go through into the stand. They usually sit behind the Directors' Box."

"The door is always locked?"

"Always. That's a firm rule."

"I'd like to have a word with McEwan. Then I'll see the referee and linesmen. They'll want to get away."

Allison turned to the commissionaire.

"When you go down find McEwan and ask him to step in here."

The man went out. Allison turned to a large cupboard facing his desk, and opened a door.

"Care for a drink, Inspector? I can do with a spot myself."

They had finished their drinks when there was a rap on the door and a short, red-faced man with a level stare entered.

"Oh, Punch," said Allison, "Inspector Slade wants to ask you a few questions."

One of McEwan's hands rubbed along the seam of his leather apron. He looked inquiringly at the Yard man.

"Were you up in the laundry during the first half, McEwan?" asked Slade.

"I was—until about twenty minutes before half-time."

"When did you return?"

"Must have been just before the whistle went. I saw the lads come back from the game for a quick cup of tea."

Slade glanced inquiringly at Allison.

"He means the players who were watching the game," the Arsenal manager explained.

"Yes, I see," nodded the detective, and turned to the laundry-man again. "Now, how long did you remain up there during the second half?"

"Oh, till the game was over. I had plenty to do."

"Then you would know if anyone came back to the training wing through the laundry, using the door to the main stand?"

Punch McEwan's square head nodded vigorously.

"Oh, aye. But no one did come through. I know that for sure. The lads went through and locked the door after them. No one came through again until they all came back at the end of the game."

"You are certain of that?" pressed Slade.

"Positive."

"Good. That's what I wanted to know. Now"—the detective turned again to Allison—"I'll have a word with the referee and linesmen."

He interviewed the three officials in Tom Whittaker's small office, but although they proved willing to help him, none of them had anything to tell that materially added to his knowledge of the case. The referee's back had been to Doyce when he fell. He was watching the ball, which was travelling into the Trojan half. The linesmen too had been watching the ball.

When Slade rejoined Allison the Arsenal manager was speaking to Kindilett.

"What next, Inspector?"

Slade smiled. He knew that this probing investigation was a real ordeal for George Allison, and he appreciated the cordial co-operation he was receiving.

"I'd like to make a rapid tour of the Stadium, if that is not asking too much."

"It isn't, if you mean the East Stand only," said Allison, with a smile.

"Yes. I was forgetting the West Stand. I think we'd better continue to forget it for the time being," Slade grinned.

It took nearly twenty-five minutes for Slade to walk over the East Stand, following the main corridors, poking into the restaurants and tea-rooms, the Press rooms and the broadcasting boxes, getting the geography of that vast wing, with offices and boardroom ending a corridor that spanned the top of the main staircase. Slade was shown how the narrow staircase from the dressing-room led up to the gymnasium, on one side, and to the laundry on the other. He was shown how by the same staircase he could enter the boardroom from the farther end. There, on the large table, flanked with tall green-leather chairs, he saw the team's strategy board, and he followed closely Allison's explanation of how, before each match, the team work out field problems.

"A pep talk does the boys some good. They go on the field feeling ready to tackle the first problem, and often it is the first problem that counts most."

From the boardroom Slade was led back to Allison's office. Outside he found Clinton talking to Irvin, the finger-prints man.

"Well, Clinton?"

The sergeant fingered his jaw.

"I don't think we're going to make much out of what Irvin's got in his bag," he said.

"Well, take good care of my tie-pin," smiled Allison. "I'm rather partial to it. You want me to arrange anything else for you, Inspector?" he asked, glancing at Slade.

"Not just now, thanks. I'll 'phone through for the ambulance, see the body taken away, and then we'll be moving off. I'm very grateful for your co-operation, Mr Allison."

For a moment Allison did not speak. His face was grave.

"I want to be of whatever assistance to the police I can, Inspector. But there's bound to be a lot of publicity about this affair—"

He hesitated.

Slade said, "I'll try to save you as much annoyance as I can, in the circumstances. I quite understand how you are placed, Mr Allison."

"Thanks, Inspector. That lets me breathe a little easier. In return, anything I can do, you know—"

They left it unexpressed, but both men had a very clear idea of just how he could expect future co-operation from the other. Slade had to make progress on a case that would be filling the national Press. Allison had to keep a large sports organization running as though nothing had happened, and as though the police were not interested in every person in the building.

There would have to be tact on both sides, and perhaps more give and take than either man realized at the moment. But each man's instinctive liking of the other boded well for harmony of working.

"I don't envy Allison his job just now," grunted Clinton as the Yard men walked down the staircase together after Slade had put through his call for the ambulance.

Apparently choosing a thought at random, Slade said, "How would you like to sniff some sea air to-morrow?"

Clinton's eyes narrowed.

"Where?"

"On the Downs near Brighton."

"Suits me," said the sergeant, "as long as we don't have to wear out our legs."

"No, I don't think we'll do that. But we may have to come back to London in a hurry."

Clinton threw his superior a quick glance. He recognized that drawled, reflexive note in Slade's voice. After working with Slade for a number of years he had come to know the other man's personal reactions to a case. He knew what that reflexive tone meant. Slade was already fitting together several of the loose pieces they had found, and expecting to find something else, as a result.

"That'll suit me," said Clinton.

The ambulance arrived. The Yard men watched the white-coated stretcher-bearers carry Doyce's body from the Arsenal Stadium. A group of curious people clustered round the entrance, kept back by a couple of policemen. The rear door of the ambulance slammed. It moved off, and at the corner of Avenell Road they heard its bell pealing shrilly.

"And now?" asked Clinton, without looking at Slade's frowning face.

"I'll put through another call to the Yard, Clinton. I'm anxious to lose no time in tracing a girl who employs purple lipstick and a peroxide bottle."

If Clinton found the reason more than a trifle obscure, he gave no sign.

"Then we'll visit Baker Street," Slade added.

V

Belloge Court

BELLOGE COURT IS ONE OF THOSE NEW BLOCKS OF FLATS SET well back from the footwalk of the main thoroughfare that seem to be the hallmark of domestic architecture of the nineteen-thirties. That Belloge Court chanced to be in Baker Street had nothing to do with its design; there had been no attempt to capture the spirit of the neighbourhood in the garish pile of fancy brick and over-bright tile.

It had achieved the forecourt of its kind, with sundry beds of wilting daffodils, apologetically nodding over clumps of dusty aubrietia. Gilt paint flaked on its railings, and low-slung cars were parked on its oil-stained concrete.

The police car in which Slade and Clinton had driven from Highbury turned in at the left-hand gilt gate. The two detectives approached the entrance hall, a blaze of light. In the midst of this brilliance, like some prisoner moth, a porter stood reading an evening paper. He looked inquiringly at the newcomers, as though he would note their faces. He was a tall man in blue uniform with brass buttons, and the peaked cap on his head was perched at a jaunty angle.

"We're from Scotland Yard," Slade announced. "I want to be shown the flat of Mr John Doyce."

For just an instant the line of the porter's jaw slackened. Then it tightened again. He folded the paper slowly.

"I saw he got crocked at the match, but—" He paused, searching the detectives' faces. He did not seem in the least perturbed by their presence. "What's wrong?" he demanded. "Don't tell me—"

"I won't," snapped Slade quickly. "Now, then, which is his flat?"

The man looked nettled for a moment. But apparently he was a philosopher of parts. He shrugged, lifting his eyebrows.

"I'll show you his flat," he said mildly. "Funny, though, his young lady didn't say something serious had happened, when she came in."

The words brought Slade facing round again.

"What's that? Who came in?"

The porter's mildness became excessive. "Why, Mr Doyce's young lady. Very pretty girl. Haven't seen her about long, but then none of them last with him—really last, I mean."

Slade perceived the faint twinkle deep in the man's blue eyes, and realized that he had assessed him too quickly.

"Is she here now?" he asked.

"No. She came down after about half an hour."

"Anything with her?"

"A small suitcase."

"She said nothing, I suppose?"

"Not a word."

"All right—er—"

"Milligan's the name, sir."

"Well, Milligan, can you describe her?"

The porter pursed his mouth. "About five foot five, I should say. Blonde—nice hair—really nice, I mean. Done in a page-boy bob."

"You use your eyes. Anything else?"

Milligan's teeth showed in a grin. "Plenty. She walks with a trip, if you know what I mean. Light on her feet, like a boxer. And she wears smart clothes. Little fussy hats—"

"Fussy hats?"

"Yes, fussy," repeated the millinery expert firmly. "With veils and bobbing things. In fact, she looks like a drawing in a woman's fashion magazine."

"You read women's fashion magazines?" said Slade sceptically.

"I get about one a day somebody or other leaves lying around the place," was the urbane reply. "Don't know that I read them, but I certainly look through them. I like looking at pretty women."

Behind him Slade heard Clinton clear his throat with a sound like a rasp biting into soft iron.

"In that case," said Slade, "you may be able to tell me the colour lipstick this young lady uses."

"Sure I can," was the ready response. "Cyclamen. New shade out. Oh, I tell you, she's an up-to-the-minute article. Chic is the word they use in the fashion books."

"I don't doubt it. What is her name?"

"Ah, that's something I can't tell you—"

"Can't?"

"Because I don't know it. I've only seen her around"—his mouth pursed again—"oh, a week I should say. Not more."

"Was she here yesterday?"

The porter grinned. "Yes, when that trainer laddie turned up—Raille, that's his name. He and I had a chat earlier in the week. Shouldn't like his job, hopping round seeing his players are fit."

"What time was this?"

"About half-past ten."

"In the evening?"

"Sure, Doyce doesn't have callers in the morning."

"He won't now," said Slade brusquely. "He's dead."

But if he expected some enlightening reaction on the part of the porter at this startling announcement he was disappointed. Milligan contented himself with a sage nod of the head.

"You can't burn the candle both ends and still live to blow it out," he said.

Slade did not query the essential truth of this declamation.

"I'd like to see the flat now," he told the man.

A lift shot them up to the fourth floor, and the porter escorted them along a green-distempered corridor.

"Number 17," he announced. "Here we are."

He stood back, perfectly willing to see Scotland Yard go into action.

"Key," Slade suggested.

"Oh."

A large bunch of pass-keys was produced, one selected and fitted into the lock. The door swung in.

"I'll probably want another word with you, Milligan, before I leave. That'll be all now."

With obvious reluctance the porter withdrew. Clinton closed the door with more force than was mechanically necessary.

"Nice place," he gave his verdict, glancing round at the airy rooms and light-coloured walls. "Hallo. Here's the harem."

On top of a walnut bureau was a pile of photographs. They were all of women. Most of them were displaying teeth that were depressingly faultless. All of them had signed her likeness. Tina and Pearl and Lottie had without stint given their love to John darling, or John dearest, or darlingest John.

"Quite a little worker," grunted Clinton, considering the implication of that group of photographs from the detached standpoint of a comfortably married man with a family.

"Looks as though the lady with the royal hue in lipsticks was anxious to leave no clue to her recent visits," said Slade. "All right, let's get to work."

The two Yard men went through the flat with a fine-toothed comb. They unlocked drawers and found letters. All were extravagantly affectionate.

"He certainly had a way with him," said Clinton.

Slade took from his pocket the pasted-up Press cutting he had found in the dead man's clothes.

"You know, Clinton," he said, "it begins to look as though a woman's behind Doyce's death. This cutting means a good deal more now we've come here. And Morring told me Doyce played a nimble game with female hearts."

"Had Doyce poached on his preserves?"

"What I thought. He said Doyce and he made it a rule to keep out of each other's social life."

Clinton snorted. "So they ended up in the same football team. Sounds likely."

"Morring admitted he didn't want Doyce in the team."

"He may be smart."

Slade was going through a well-stocked wardrobe. "True. You're remembering the ten thousand pounds I told you about in the car."

"It fits together."

Clinton was one of those people who believe in direct action and clear-cut opinions. He preferred to empty his mind of extraneous irrelevancies and examine what was left. It was a sound method of investigation. It kept the thinker's feet where they should be, on the ground. Slade well knew the value to himself of Clinton's downright tactics and forthright arguing.

"And this blonde. Where does she fit in?" he asked the sergeant.

Clinton lifted his head from the depths of a travelling-trunk, the contents of which appeared to be old pyjama suits, tattered paper-bound novels, and an assortment of discarded top clothes.

"She doesn't—yet."

"She was at the match," Slade pointed out.

"Not unusual. Doyce probably paraded his physical fitness and prowess. Women fall for that line. Besides, that cutting isn't recent."

The last point was one that had been troubling Slade since he had searched the dead man's clothes.

"If I'm not wrong it's older than any of those photos, Clinton."

The sergeant squatted on his haunches, turned over an old pair of flannel trousers and felt in the pockets.

"Does that tell us anything?" he inquired.

"Perhaps not now—but I'm hoping. Among the pins you collected and Irvin took back to the Yard, did you have anything out of the ordinary?"

"No. Tie-pins, drawing-pins, a needle or two—nothing much. Not all of it would fit into that small envelope we found, but I thought we might as well have the lot tested. Be a bit of a jolt if he died of heart failure, after all."

Slade found a book of cuttings. They were all descriptions of matches in which Doyce had played. The references to Doyce were underlined in green ink. Judging by the critics of soccer, the dead man had been one of the best half-backs in the country. "A brilliant, stylistic player," said one writer, "John Doyce was easily

the most accomplished half-back on the field. He held the Rovers
like a keystone holds an arch. Again and again the crowd cheered
his efforts. Times without number after attacking he fell back to
extricate the Rovers' defence from the folds of a clever opposing
forward line."

Slade glanced at the date.

It was four years before. He could not find the name of the
newspaper.

"Clinton, got that programme of this afternoon's match?"

The sergeant took the red-covered Arsenal v. Trojans programme from his pocket and gave it to Slade, who opened it at
the column headed "Our Visitors." In black type were the names
of the Trojan players. After each name were some details of the
player's career.

Slade found that three of the players—namely, Setchley, Doyce,
and Morring—had all at one time been members of a team called
the Saxon Rovers.

"Look, Clinton," he pointed out. "This is interesting. These
three players were each in the same team to-day. Some time ago
they were in another team together. Two of them are business
partners, the other is a research chemist. One of the business
partners is dead, poisoned by a very deadly—and I believe unusual—poison. How does that begin to look to you?"

"Something's rotten in the State of Denmark," said Clinton
heavily. "But you haven't worked the mysterious blonde into it,"
he added, with a sly dig.

Slade grinned wryly.

"I haven't, have I?" He gave his attention again to the programme. "You know, Clinton, I think we're going to find ourselves
up against a rather subtle plot."

Clinton grunted and looked dour.

"Book-writers to the contrary, I don't think there's anything subtle in poisoning a man. And with ten thousand pounds ready to slip across the table—"

He turned away without completing the words.

"You think it's as open-and-shut as that," said Slade.

Clinton turned.

"No. I don't think that," he said slowly. "But I do think Morring will have a lot more to tell us—later."

"How do you mean—later?"

"Just that," replied the sergeant doggedly. "A man who doesn't want his business partner in the same team as himself has a very special reason for keeping away from him. Especially when they have played in another team together."

Slade realized that behind Clinton's words lay the vague outline of an idea which the sergeant was turning over in his mind. Clinton believed strongly in visual and first-hand evidence. It was his stock argument that nine murderers out of ten were hanged solely because a detective found the obvious and read it aright.

"We'll have a further chance with Morring to-morrow, at the Dyke Golf Club," Slade reminded him. "Hallo—nearly time for the news," he broke off, glancing at his watch.

He crossed to a radio in the sitting-room and switched it on. They waited some moments before the time signal sounded, and then the announcer said, "There is a police message before the news. The police are anxious to get in touch with a young woman who called at the Arsenal Stadium this afternoon after the match and asked to see Mr John Doyce. Will the person concerned please call at any police station or communicate with Scotland Yard, telephone number Whitehall 1212? We regret to announce that

John Doyce has since died. An account of the match will be given in the late sports bulletin—"

Slade switched off. The voice faded.

Twenty minutes later the two Yard men had completed their search. They had found little. Clinton stood in the middle of the living-room, looking glumly about him.

"I reckon that's the lot. Whoever the girl is she's covered her tracks damned well. Maybe she was a Girl Guide."

They went down to the brightly lit entrance hall. The porter saw them and came out of a glass-enclosed cage.

"Well?" he said, as though he expected an explanation.

"Listen, Milligan," said Slade. "If that girl shows up again ring the Yard, and do your best to keep her here."

The porter's eyes kindled.

"You want her, eh?"

"I want to talk to her," Slade amended cautiously.

"I get it," nodded Milligan sagely. "You can trust me."

The two Yard men went back to their waiting car, and were sped through the evening traffic to the grey-stone, soot-smeared pile that is Scotland Yard. Slade spent a testing half-hour with the A.C., answering questions and generally outlining the case as far as he had progressed. He went back to his own office, to find Clinton with his nose buried in a newspaper.

"Any news?" asked the sergeant, folding the paper and putting it on one side.

"No. The District Messenger angle has been covered and it gives us no lead," said Slade.

"How's that?"

"The package was handed in at an office near Victoria Station this morning, some time about ten-thirty. All we can get from the man who took the package was that the person who brought it was a man wearing a light-coloured overcoat and he remembers that the man wore a hat."

"Well, that's a help," said Clinton sarcastically. "We needn't bother with a man who doesn't own a hat—unless he borrowed one."

"Frankly, I wasn't expecting much from that lead," Slade admitted.

"You haven't been disappointed. A pale overcoat and a hat. Not even a trilby or a bowler or a pork-pie or a Homburg or a velour or a—a—"

"Topper?"

Clinton scowled. "Just a hat," he complained. "My God! What do people use their eyes for?"

"You'd be surprised," Slade told him. He picked up a 'phone and was put through to the Police Laboratory. For a couple of minutes he asked questions, then hung up. "Well, Clinton, a few other wheels are turning. They've already started work on Doyce and those pins you collected. I don't think we can do much till to-morrow. We'll get down to the golf club early."

Clinton picked up a paper and handed it to Slade.

"Meadows' report."

Slade glanced over the sheet of small handwriting. It all boiled down to confirmation of what the police surgeon had told Slade in the Arsenal dressing-room. Meadows was of the opinion that Doyce had died from alkaloid poisoning, and that the poison had been introduced into his system subcutaneously.

"All right, slip it in the file."

Slade passed the sheet back to his assistant. Clinton dropped it into a folder on which he had already printed in large letters "Arsenal Stadium Case."

"No news of the girl?"

"Not yet. Give her time."

"My idea," said Clinton, "is that she won't come forward."

"You gave me that idea at the flat."

"Girls seem to be mixed up in this affair pretty—"

"The cutting?" Slade interrupted.

"Yes," nodded the sergeant, "that's what I was thinking of. That was about a girl—a dead girl."

Slade took a turn across the room.

"I've arranged with the A.C.," he told his assistant, "to have that cutting circulated in the provinces. It'll be photographed and printed and sent to every police station. There's a chance we can find the paper—a slim one, but a chance."

Clinton rose. "I suppose that does cover everything," he said. "Well, I can do with some sleep. You coming?"

"Not for half an hour. I want to go through those notes you've taken. Where's the book?"

Clinton took his notebook from his pocket and dropped it on Slade's desk.

"Then I'll say good night."

"Good night," said Slade.

The door closed after the sergeant. Slade took out his pipe and lit it. He sat down and from the "Arsenal Stadium Case" file took the red-covered programme. He turned to "Our Visitors" and again read the notes on Morring, Doyce, and Setchley.

There was a connecting thread between them, he knew. They had all played in the same team previously, and—

But he was going over old ground, and he found nothing new, nothing he had not seen before. On a fresh page of Clinton's notebook he found the addresses and telephone numbers of the

Trojan team, taken by the sergeant at the Stadium. He picked up the 'phone and asked the operator to get him Morring's number. A few minutes later he heard Morring's voice.

"Sorry to bother you at this hour," said Slade, "but there was something I wanted to ask you."

"Well?"

The word was vaguely truculent.

"Was Doyce engaged?"

"Not to my knowledge."

"Had he any special lady friend of the moment?"

"Probably a dozen. Does that answer your question?"

Slade sighed.

"Since you ask—no. Good night."

The line went dead.

VI

Cherchez La Femme

A CAR CLIMBED OVER THE DOWNS AND JOINED A STEADY stream of traffic. Slade, who was driving, changed down.

"We haven't got the place to ourselves," he remarked.

Clinton stared at the traffic.

"Amazing where cars get to these days. You'd think they'd all be in Brighton."

"Perhaps these are inhabitants, not Londoners," Slade suggested. "Just giving over the town to the invader."

The column of cars picked up speed. Slade turned off to the right and climbed a road that led to a cleared parking-space. Opposite, built on higher ground, was the club-house of the Dyke Golf Club.

George Allison and Francis Kindilett were seated inside. They rose as the two Yard men entered.

"Nice morning," said Kindilett.

"Bit of a breeze," Clinton thought.

Allison took Slade aside.

"I've fixed up that game for you with Morring," he said.

"Good," nodded the Yard man. "Where is he?"

"Outside. Come with me."

The Arsenal manager led Slade to where Morring sat reading a magazine. The Trojan back rose, nodded, and picked up his clubs.

Allison looked questioningly at Slade, who grinned and made off after the footballer.

They teed off. Slade, talking about conventional trivialities, strove to thaw his companion's cold moroseness. By the time they had reached the third green Slade's tactics were beginning to show some slight result.

"You know," said the detective, "I know a man who can never make up his mind whether it's possible to have too much life insurance or too little. I was wondering how you, as an insurance broker, felt. Of course, your job is to sell insurance, so—"

"Oh, I don't advocate anyone getting in too deep," said Morring. "It all depends upon the individual's circumstances. Life insurance can be an excellent form of investment, locking up capital that can appreciate until such time as it's required."

"Now take this man I mentioned…"

Slade, having got his man started, saw to it that he didn't run down like a piece of clockwork. Subtly he swung from insurance to football, keeping away from yesterday's tragedy, and from football to men who followed the game. Another switch to men who combined football and an everyday job introduced the Trojans, as examples, and Doyce was mentioned incidentally.

But the Yard man, watching his man closely, saw that he was not ready to talk freely about Doyce. Morring shied from mention of his dead partner, changed the conversation quickly.

"Look," he pointed ahead. "Hapgood, the Arsenal captain, playing Chulley, our captain. Getting back to your friend who is worried about insurance, Inspector…"

Slade found himself where he had started. They were on the home stretch when Slade saw a figure hurrying towards them. Allison came up, flourishing a magazine.

"Look!" he said excitedly. "I've found her."

He pointed to a page of the magazine. It held the picture of a girl sitting up in bed reaching for a cigarette. She was a pretty girl, and the pose she had struck was calculatedly alluring.

"The girl—the girl!" said Allison, as Slade stared at the picture, making no comment. "The girl who called to see Doyce at the Stadium."

"This is her?"

"Absolutely positive. Couldn't be mistaken."

Slade continued to stare at the picture.

"A photographer's model, and she hasn't come forward yet."

"Did you expect her to?" asked Morring.

Slade faced the speaker. Morring's face looked flushed and his eyes were narrowed.

"There was a police SOS for her on the radio last night," said Slade. "Usually people come forward in response to such appeals—if they've got nothing to hide."

"What could she have to hide?" Morring demanded.

"I don't know," said Slade. "She called at the Stadium, asked for Doyce, and ran off when she heard the police were on the way. I later discovered that she had visited Doyce at his flat the night before."

Morring turned quickly away, but not before Slade had caught the sudden wild gleam under his down-drawn lids.

"How can you be sure it's the same girl?" he asked gruffly.

"Mr Allison recognizes her. The porter at Doyce's flat described her. You didn't by any chance know her?"

It was a direct challenge. Morring had to face it.

"Me? Good Lord, I didn't know any of—of the women Doyce favoured! Are we going to finish the game?"

"Of course. See you back at the club-house," Slade nodded to Allison.

The Arsenal manager glanced from one man to the other.

"I'll be there," he said, slipping the magazine into his pocket.

When they reached the eighteenth hole Morring made his excuses and hurried away. Slade followed more slowly to the club-house.

"Morring come in here?" he asked Allison, who was seated next to Kindilett, drinking a whisky.

"No." Allison took out his magazine, opened it to the page showing the girl. "You'd better take this, Inspector. You can check up on her."

"Who?" inquired Kindilett.

"This girl," said Slade. "She called at the Stadium yesterday, asked for Doyce, and then ran off. I later found she'd visited Doyce at his flat."

"May I see?"

Slade held out the magazine.

Kindilett gave the picture one glance and sat upright. "There must be some mistake. That's Morring's fiancée—Pat Laruce!"

"You're sure?" said the Yard man, recovering quickly from this startling announcement.

"Why, of course I am!" said Kindilett testily. "Everyone in the team knows Pat."

Slade's glance found Allison's. The Yard man's eyes flashed warning signals. The Arsenal manager nodded in understanding.

"Well, I'm afraid I can't stop for a drink, gentlemen," said the Yard man. "I've got a call to make."

"The telephone's that way," said Kindilett, pointing.

"Thanks."

Slade was in time to see Morring leave the club's 'phone-booth. The footballer ran out of the club-house and made for the car-park.

Clinton appeared as from nowhere.

"You look in a hurry."

"I am. Morring's just put through a call, and unless I miss my guess he's ready to lead us straight to the girl we want to see."

"How do you figure that out?" asked the sergeant.

"He's engaged to her. Come on. Keep behind this row of cars. I don't want him to see us."

They reached their own car as another car moved out of the row and turned down the road. Seated at the wheel was Morring. His face was set, his eyes stared straight ahead.

"Certainly looks as though he's got something on his mind," grunted Clinton.

"It hit him between the eyes when Allison produced the girl's photo and I said she'd been at Doyce's flat. But the reason didn't register till Kindilett saw the picture and recognized her."

"Which picture?"

"Here."

Slade pushed the magazine, opened at the page showing the girl reaching for a cigarette, into Clinton's hands, and started the car. He drove out of the row and turned down the road, a hundred yards behind Morring.

"She's a good looker," Clinton decided. "So she's been playing tricks, eh?"

"Looks like it." Slade braked and gave way to an oncoming car. "Morring's steamed up."

"Because we know."

Slade was silent for some moments. Finally he said, "Perhaps."

"He knew about her and Doyce. Bet your boots on that." Clinton saw no two ways about the thing. "This just about fixes him."

The sergeant settled back, lit a cigarette.

"Ten thousand quid plus a girl. He'll have to be good to talk himself out of that set-up." Clinton's exhaled smoke mushroomed against the windscreen. "Somehow I don't think he's that good," he added, a doleful note in his voice.

Slade turned on to the main road across the Downs. There was still plenty of traffic about, and he couldn't make a good speed, but he was able to keep the same distance between his car and Morring's. Traffic lights at a junction let Morring turn to the left and speed away towards the London road, but Slade edged to the front of the grouped cars when the lights turned again. There were four cars between him and Morring when the lights went red at the London road.

"You're going to have your work cut out," said Clinton, throwing away the butt of his cigarette.

If anything, that was a measure of understatement. Morring drove fast, and he handled his car expertly. Only good luck enabled Slade to remain at his quarry's heels when Morring swung on to the Purley by-pass. The level crossing at Crawley had been closed after Slade had bumped over the metals. The lights at Redhill had changed as he slipped over the cross-roads.

Within sight of London, Morring apparently put a restraining hand on his flight. He slackened speed. Through Norbury and Streatham he almost dawdled.

"Why's he slowing up?" muttered Clinton. "Losing heart?"

"Or nerve," Slade suggested.

Morring passed through South London, crossed the Thames at Vauxhall, went on through Victoria, by Hyde Park Corner, and

turned along the Edgware Road. He led the police-car to a block
of flats in Maida Vale.

Slade drove past as Morring ran into the entrance.

"I bet he's just about ready to bite," said Clinton.

Which remark only goes to prove that the sergeant hadn't
studied human beings for the years he had without learning
something.

Morring bounded up a broad flight of stairs, sprang across a
landing, and rang a door-bell. His face was a graven mask. There
was an air of suppressed urgency about him. The fingers of his
hands flexed and closed with automatic regularity.

The door opened, revealing a girl with dark hair and wide eyes.

"Why, Phil—"

"Hallo, Jill. Pat's in?"

"Of course."

He was inside the flat, moving across the sitting-room with
springy stride. Another door opened, and a blonde girl in a silk
dressing-gown came into the room. She smiled with all the heart-
quickening charm of some one trained in the art. Her blonde hair
was perfectly set, her make-up was clever, effective. She stood,
loosely holding herself together, a picture of studied ease.

The sudden visitor glanced at the ring on her third finger. It
was a half-hoop of diamonds.

"Pat," he said, and there was an edge to his voice, "I've got to
talk to you. I've got to get some things straightened out. Jill"—he
turned to the dark-haired girl—"perhaps you'd be an angel and—"

Jill Howard nodded.

"Sure, Phil. I know when to be scarce." Her smile was quick,
but dubious. "You look as though you've brought the news from
Ghent to Aix."

He met her questioning eyes.

"I hope I've brought false news, Jill."

The blonde said, "I could do with a cigarette, Phil, and perhaps you wouldn't mind letting me in on the secret. After all, it was me you 'phoned."

Morring gave her a cigarette, held out his lighter. The inner door closed after Jill.

"Yes, Pat, I 'phoned you because there's something I've got to get straight."

"You're repeating yourself," she pointed out.

"I heard you were at Doyce's flat Friday night."

She stood for a moment smoking, watching the end of her cigarette.

"Where did you hear that?" she asked quietly.

Her very calm shook the man.

"Never mind where!" he shouted. "Is it true? That's what I want to know, and by heaven, Pat—"

"Don't be a fool, Phil." The cold, level tone was like a stinging douche of ice-water. "There's no need to get dramatic about something that has a very simple explanation."

"Simple—"

"That's what I said."

Morring's mouth screwed up at one side. "All right, I'm listening, Pat." A vein throbbed visibly in his forehead. "But if you've broken your promise—"

She cut in sharply, a keen, wary look on her face.

"I had promised to see him long before you two had that quarrel. After all, he was your partner. I—well"—she hedged—"I didn't think it policy to break the date."

"But you went back to his flat."

The words were an accusation. Cleverly she avoided their real meaning.

"Naturally I went back for a drink—there was nothing in that. Or are you suggesting—"

A new note crept into her voice, one of hesitant anger. Morring watched her from under contracted brows, and didn't know what to think. Pat was always so damnably clever. She always managed to get him...

"Listen," he said, "I didn't come here to suggest anything. I came to get the truth. The police know you're engaged to me—"

"Who told them?" she flashed.

"Well—" He hesitated. "I don't know quite—"

"Phil"—she threw the cigarette away—"I don't know what you're trying to tell me, but I can't see how the police know I exist, unless you yourself told them."

She waited.

"I didn't tell them," he denied.

"Then how can they know?"

He shook his head. "That's what puzzles me. They know you visited Doyce's flat. That Yard detective—what's his name?—Slade had a magazine with a photo of you which George Allison recognized. Slade said—"

"How does George Allison come into it?" she demanded thinly.

"You spoke to him at the Stadium. You went in and asked after Doyce."

"I see. But none of this connects with—your fiancée."

She looked at him, eyes wild, lips slightly parted. And she knew just how the sight of her hurt him, left him unsure of himself and the thoughts whirling in his mind.

He shook his head as though to clear it.

"Don't you see, Pat, the police are on your track?"

"My track?"

Her voice rose a few notes.

"Of course. I understand they radioed an S O S for a girl—you. Well, what have you done about it? Nothing. They want to question you—about Doyce. I tell you, Pat, you can't play with the police like this. You've got to watch your step."

"Why me?"

Her question brought him up short.

"What do you mean?"

"Aren't you getting just a bit scared, Phil, that the police will ask me questions about—you?"

The directness of this new attack took him aback.

"Me? They don't want me. I told Inspector Slade all I knew yesterday."

"I see. You thought of everything very nicely."

"Why, Pat, what do you mean?"

Her glance sharpened. She moved nearer him.

"You've seen to-day's papers?"

"Yes."

"Then you know how they've spread themselves about the case. The missing girl. Oh, I know the rotten suggestion behind it all! The partner who gets ten thousand pounds. But I didn't know the police had found out we were engaged."

"What difference does it make?"

She searched his face, found him honestly puzzled.

"How long do you think it'll be before a smart detective finds out about your quarrel with Doyce—and because he was paying too much attention to me? Add that to ten thousand pounds—"

"Pat!"

Morring's cry was one of outrage. He caught her by the arms, and felt how relaxed she stood. There was a mocking look about her as she stared up at him, realizing more than he realized, seeing more than he saw, and concealing from him—what?

He was filled with distrust. It suddenly seemed that he had never really known her, that she was a stranger whose thoughts he did not share, whose life was utterly outside his own.

"I'm just trying to face up to things, Phil. Trying not to be scared. We've got to be smart if we're going to side-step a lot of publicity—"

"Smart!"

He released her, fell back.

"That's what I said. Publicity of the wrong sort wouldn't do you any good. As for me"—animation suddenly flowed through her, a vibrant note echoed in her voice—"I can't afford that kind if I'm going to keep my job. Don't you see, Phil? We've got to—to be not—engaged. The police wouldn't understand. You and John—that money—me. They mustn't be told, Phil. You mustn't tell them we're engaged. You mustn't!"

She was close against him now, arms lifted to fold round his neck.

He caught her wrists.

"I'm beginning to see things clearly," he said.

She caught at the words.

"What do you mean?" she demanded. "Phil"—with a gesture of tired exasperation—"why try to blunder about at the wrong time? Can't you see—"

He picked up his hat.

"I think—perfectly. Good-bye."

Before she could stop him he had reached the door and opened it. He stopped abruptly. On the landing, conversing in low tones, were Slade and Clinton. At sound of the door opening both Yard men turned round.

"Ah, Mr Morring," said Slade, smiling.

Morring gulped.

"What the devil—" he began, stopped.

"We would just like to ask you a few more questions, and also Miss—er—Laruce, is it?" said Slade pleasantly, turning his smile to the blonde woman standing behind Morring.

VII

Not the Whole Truth

JILL STOOD IN THE CENTRE OF THE SITTING-ROOM. SHE watched Clinton close the door.

"I didn't know we were having company, Pat. You might have told me."

Pat forced a smile.

"Friends of Phil's, I think, dear."

Morring's head jerked up. He had been staring at Pat's left hand. His engagement ring had disappeared from her third finger. He had the feeling that Pat was far too capable—in looking after herself.

"Allow me to introduce Inspector Slade and Sergeant—Sorry, I didn't catch the name yesterday."

"Clinton," said the sergeant dourly.

"Oh!" Pat sounded as though she had made a discovery. "I know. You're investigating John Doyce's death. I saw your names in the paper this morning. That's right, isn't it?"

Slade nodded. "Yes. You knew Doyce rather well, didn't you, Miss Laruce?"

She appeared surprised.

"I knew him as Phil—er—Mr Morring's business partner. Did you expect me to know him well?"

Slade admired her cool counter-attack. She was very self-assured.

"To be frank, I did. That's why I'm here. I was hoping you would be able to tell me something that might be useful in my investigation."

"Sorry to disappoint you, Inspector," she said with a too-sweet smile. "But what are you investigating—exactly?"

Slade studied her carefully.

"I expect to know later. Just now I am investigating a death in somewhat strange circumstances." He turned his head as a chair scraped along the floor. The other girl had sat down. "Can you help me?"

Pat shook her head with pretty bewilderment.

"Why, of course, if I could, I'd be delighted. But, really, what makes you think I know anything about—I mean anything that could help you?"

Morring was standing with mouth shut tight, a brooding look on his face. He made no motion to interrupt the verbal duel between the Yard man and the girl.

"You called at the Stadium after the match. You asked to see Doyce?"

"What makes you so certain, Inspector?"

"You were recognized."

She caught her lip. "True I did ask. It was only natural, wasn't it?"

"I don't know."

A slow flush crept into her face.

"I mean in the circumstances."

"Which circumstances?"

"Well—John being Phil's partner—and my knowing them both. Being friends, I mean. Yes, that's what I mean."

Slade glanced at Jill. The other girl was sitting still, staring at the floor as though puzzled by the pattern of the carpet.

"Why didn't you come forward when the request for you was broadcast last night?"

"I didn't hear the broadcast, Inspector. I didn't know until a short while ago, when I saw about the police S O S in the paper. I had intended getting in touch with the police when I was dressed, though there's nothing I can tell that could possibly be of any use."

Slade accepted this for what he considered it was worth, which wasn't a great deal.

"Miss Laruce," said the detective, with an air of coming to the point, "tell me, please, why you went to Doyce's flat as soon as you left the Stadium."

Pat gasped, looked from Slade to Clinton, and shook her head.

"But I don't understand. Do you mean you think I went to his flat—alone?"

"I do."

She drew herself up to her full height, which wasn't much more than five foot five, but she managed somehow to make the movement censorious.

"Then I can tell you, Inspector, you are mistaken—very much mistaken. I did not go to Doyce's flat. I came straight back here—didn't I, Jill?"

Thus appealed to, the other girl started. She threw one wild glance round, found Morring's puzzled gaze on her, met Slade's hard stare, crossed Clinton's unwavering scowl, and lastly looked at Pat. The blonde girl stood in the centre of the room waiting for her roommate's confirmation, expecting it, as her attitude showed.

Jill swallowed quickly.

"Why, of course, Pat. We came back together."

"Straight from the Stadium?" snapped Slade.

"Straight back from the Stadium," said Jill, more colour in her tone.

Slade sighed.

"Strange. The porter at the flats must have been mistaken, Clinton."

"Must have been. But I don't see how," said the sergeant, taking out his notebook and producing a pencil.

"What are you putting down?" asked Pat sharply.

"Notes—just notes," said Clinton, without bothering to look up.

"I may have to ask you to make an official statement later," said Slade.

"About what?"

"About what you've just told me."

"Oh."

There was an awkward pause. Clinton went on with his writing, Morring fidgeted, and Jill sat crouching in her chair, watching them all rather fearfully.

"Miss Laruce is your fiancée, I believe, Mr Morring," said Slade, turning to the footballer.

"That's—" began Morring.

"Really, Inspector, you are embarrassing me," put in the girl quickly. "If Phil wants to ask me to become engaged to him I don't want to have to thank Scotland Yard for prompting him."

Over by the door Clinton choked.

"I'm sorry," said Slade, but he was looking at Morring. Surprise was mingled with anger in the man's face. "Then you are not engaged to him?"

She carried it off exceedingly well. She said, "We are excellent friends of long standing, but now you have made such a suggestion—Well."

A slow flush burned in Morring's face. The man's eyes were glassy, masking a low-tension fury.

"It seems I have been getting some wrong ideas about people," said Slade dryly.

"It certainly does," Pat agreed warmly.

The Yard man turned to Jill.

"Did you know John Doyce well, Miss—"

"Howard—Jill Howard. No, I have seen him only once or twice."

"Then you were not friends?"

"No, I am rather particular about my friends."

There was a wealth of contempt in her tone. Pat's lips compressed. She gave no other sign that the shaft had struck home.

"Then you did not like him?"

"I did not think anything about him."

"What did you know about him?"

"He was Phil's partner, that's all."

"But his reputation—social reputation?"

"He was a good footballer, of course."

"That wasn't what I meant. Had he a reputation that would interest a woman?"

"Surely that would depend on the woman, Inspector?"

Slade was getting no change from this slim dark-haired girl with the bright hostile eyes.

"Listen, Inspector," said Morring, coming forward, "you don't have to plague Miss Howard like this. I told you about my partner yesterday."

"For which I was very grateful," returned Slade easily. "But I am open to receive every one's opinion. Opinions differ, you know. You agree, Miss Laruce?"

"Naturally."

Pat sat down, crossed one leg over the other. She was undeniably pretty.

"What was your opinion of Mr Doyce?" Slade asked her.

She wriggled in the chair.

"Why, I always found him very pleasant. I—er—"

"Yes?"

"I can't find anything else to say. People always will talk."

Slade didn't ask what she meant. He could see that, without any aid from himself, Morring was working into a furious temper about something. With great difficulty the man kept check on his temper.

"You are a photographer's model, I believe?"

"I am."

"Mind letting me have your firm's address?"

"I can't think why you want it, but I don't mind. Why should I? The Commer-Photo Agency, Ltd., 10 Langdale House, Regent Street."

Clinton noted the information.

"And you, Miss Howard?"

"My daily bread comes much more prosaically," smiled the dark girl. "I'm behind the counter in the gift department of Farnham and Macey's."

Clinton noted that too.

Slade turned to Morring. "You came here rather suddenly, Mr Morring."

"You find that interesting?" countered the footballer, wary and on his guard.

"Frankly, I do."

"Then I'm sorry. I can't satisfy your interest, Inspector."

"Perhaps you will reconsider that, Mr Morring, when you sign a statement for me. But I shan't be pressing you for that until to-morrow."

There was an ironic curve to Morring's mouth as he asked, "Why wait?"

"I think it better that I get a report from the experts performing the *post-mortem*—first."

Morring had dropped his guard, and Slade had given him one right between the eyes. The footballer looked staggered.

"Then you think—you really do—I mean, what I said to you yesterday—"

He floundered to a stop.

Pat said, "You look as though you could do with a cup of coffee, Phil. It's the excitement. Jill, won't you be an angel?"

Jill retired to the kitchen to perform her requested heavenly duties.

"And won't you both sit down?" Pat invited the detectives sweetly.

Slade, quite prepared to see how this rather clever young woman was going to continue what he was sure was nothing but a big bluff, selected a chair. Morring slumped into another, opposite.

"And you, sergeant?"

Clinton stowed his notebook in his pocket.

"Thanks, but I'll stand, miss. It's a long run from Brighton, and I can do with stretching my legs."

"Brighton?"

"We were there this morning," said Slade. "Mr Morring and I played golf."

"But what fun! You like golf, Inspector?"

Clinton cleared his throat noisily. He could see all this developing into a social call of the kind he detested. Slade grinned.

"I'm afraid neither Mr Morring nor I had all our mind on the game," he said bluntly.

Morring squirmed.

"Pat," he said, "I don't think I'll wait for that coffee. There's something I've just thought of—"

"Well, just forget it again, there's a darling." A white hand with pink shellaced nails pressed him down into his seat. "You can't run out on us after coming all the way from Brighton just to keep a date with Jill and me."

"I—" Morring gulped.

"I'm sorry," Slade apologized. "I wouldn't have kept you to that game, Mr Morring, if I'd known."

It was Clinton's turn to grin. The sergeant made no attempt to hide his amusement. Morring flushed, ran a finger round the inside of his collar, and nodded.

"Oh, it was all right. I had plenty of time—"

"You certainly got here before the lady was dressed," Clinton pointed out.

The situation was deteriorating. It was saved from disaster by the entry of Jill with a tray of steaming coffee-cups.

"Now, who takes sugar?"

"Were you in the Saxon Rovers at the same time as Setchley and Doyce?" asked Slade, while Clinton played at legerdemain with a pair of patent sugar-tongs.

"Yes. That was four years ago, though."

"So I understand. Any others of the Trojan team in the Rovers?"

"Kindilett was a member of the Committee. That's how he knew about us when he started the Trojans. He turned to some of his old players, got us interested."

"Setchley been a player long?"

"As long as I have, I should say. He's a queer fellow. Scientific outlook. Doesn't give a fig for human values. Much more concerned with the result than the game." Morring set his cup in its saucer. "If it's news to you, he was the one who rooted for Doyce. Said the team really needed him as right half."

Slade didn't say whether it was news or not. He nodded and asked, "Setchley married?"

"No."

"Engaged?"

Morring frowned. "No. Any reason for asking?"

"I've always a reason," Slade explained mildly.

"Sorry. But—" Morring hesitated, unsure of himself.

"Inspector Slade's very interested in the ladies," said Pat, "if you know what I mean."

Jill's cup smacked loudly against its saucer.

"I'm not sure I do," said Slade.

Pat smiled provocatively. "The great big detective wouldn't fool a poor little girl, would he?" she purred, completely at ease.

Slade grinned, quite aware of her effort to sidetrack him, but not sure just why. He didn't think she was helping Morring. He didn't think she really cared much for anybody except herself.

Probably even Doyce had been...

He didn't allow speculation to wander far in that direction. It was too risky, and he had to see exactly where he was getting.

"I'm hoping the poor little girl won't turn the tables on the detective," he said.

Something went wrong with the smile she gave him, but her tone was light when she said, "Just to show you what a wrong idea you've got of me, Inspector, I'll be perfectly frank with you."

Slade sat back, wondering what verbal trick she would try to pull.

"You think John Doyce was murdered—poisoned. Oh, never mind! I can read between the lines of the Sunday Press. When I say you I mean the police, naturally." In that way she brushed aside his quick but cautious denial. "You think a woman is mixed up in this business because you've heard some rumours about Doyce—rumours you were bound to run into, because no one would try to whiten his reputation when he is dead."

"Pat!"

The cry came from Jill. But the blonde girl swept on, warmth in her voice.

"You've tried to connect me with the case. You've considered Jill. Now you want to drag in Setchley—if he has a girl friend. Because, like every one else, you think Doyce was murdered for only one reason. Women liked him."

"Good God!" muttered Jill.

Pat flashed her a glance, half savage, half elated.

"They did," she snapped. "He had only to lift his finger and women fell on his neck—"

"Pat!" It was Morring who was protesting this time. He was on his feet, angry, roused. "Do you know what you're saying? Do you know what—"

She rounded on him. "I know exactly what I'm saying." There was venom in the words. "You didn't like him, Phil. Jill here didn't like him. But I did, and I'm not ashamed to admit it."

Morring fell back before this onslaught. Slade, watching closely, wondered what the girl was trying to put over. Something, some impression, he was sure. She was acting, and for a very good reason, but he couldn't find it, and he felt frustrated.

"You visited him Friday night, didn't you?" he said easily.

The question caught her unprepared. She went down like a pricked balloon. The eagerness died from her face, the animation left her limbs. She sat slumped in the chair. Numbed was the word that flashed into Slade's mind.

"You know that too," she said quietly.

"The truth is always simpler," said Slade.

She looked at him, and her gaze was hard.

"That still doesn't make me change what I said. I wasn't in his flat yesterday evening. You heard what Jill said."

She was very angry with the detective. Her effort to conceal her anger was only partially successful. She knew, and all in the room knew, that the Yard man had subtly forced her into revealing a lie.

She had lied when she said she wasn't in Doyce's flat the previous evening. The curtain of the lie had been rent. And she had implicated Jill Howard, who had been forced reluctantly into supporting her.

"Of course you weren't," said Slade. He rose. "I think we'll be moving along, Clinton. Well, thank you, every one, for your co-operation—and the coffee. I'll be seeing you later, Mr Morring."

The two Yard men walked to the door. Jill Howard sprang forward and opened it. She followed them on to the landing outside the flat and drew the door to.

"You mustn't take much notice of Pat, Inspector," she said. "Pat's rather given to dramatizing things. You mustn't—er—expect too much from her."

"I don't," smiled Slade, and his smile vanished. "But I don't like to see a silly woman make trouble for others by demanding their loyalty—which she knows she'll get."

The dark-haired girl pressed her hands together in a quick, nervous movement.

"We understand her, Inspector."

"I don't think anyone understands a liar," said Slade uncompromisingly.

Jill's glance was pleading. "But even if she were at the flat, Inspector, it wouldn't mean anything—it couldn't. She's in love with—"

In time she caught herself from making a bad slip. Slade patted her shoulder.

"Your friend's very lucky, Miss Howard," he said, and turned away.

Clinton followed him out to the car.

"They say birds of a feather are drawn together," said the sergeant. "I reckon those two are the exception that proves the rule. That blonde would lie just to be different, and expect the other to back her up."

Slade set the car in motion. They joined the stream of traffic moving south towards the Marble Arch.

"She's very afraid of something, Clinton. Her job, Morring, us—I don't know. She put on a good act, and gave herself away at the end."

"She hasn't made things look better for Morring—on paper," Clinton pointed out. "He rushes there, and they have an obvious fight before we arrive. Then they stall, and the little dark one looks as unhappy as hell. She makes good coffee."

"If I'm not far wrong, Clinton, our golden-haired Pat has been playing the old game of matching the two ends against the middle. She denied being engaged to Morring because she doesn't know how much we have found out about her relationship with Doyce, and she's smart enough to think of appearances. Oh, she's fly, that girl. Unless Morring's careful she'll set his wandering feet on a long walk up the garden path."

"And the time may be eight o'clock in the morning," said Clinton ominously.

He looked at Slade, expecting a response.

For once he was disappointed.

VIII

Like Yeast Working

IT OCCURRED TO CLINTON AS SLADE DROVE DOWN THE
Edgware Road that there were a number of questions his
chief had not asked Morring before they left the girls' flat. Like a
chess-player testing a risky move, he said casually, "Why did we
leave when we did?"

"You think we could have got some more out of them, eh?"

"There was plenty of heat under the kettle," said the sergeant.
"It might have boiled over."

Slade smiled.

"I think it has," he said.

Clinton looked at him, understanding lighting his eyes.

"I get it. You started some trouble, left it to simmer. You think
they'll have a row, and then begin shouting. You left them with
a lot of doubts." The sergeant nodded. "Doubts that'll work like
yeast."

Clinton's literary style was rarely impeccable. More often than
not his metaphors were inextricably mixed. But despite blemishes
which might cause a pedant to frown he had a happy knack of
stating graphically what was in his mind. He was never ambigu-
ous. He was never misunderstood.

"Exactly," said Slade, in the same conversational vein. "I thought
it was time for seconds out of the ring."

Had the Yard man been an unobserved witness to the scene at that moment taking place in the flat he had recently left he would have found ample confirmation of his opinion.

With the departure of the detectives Morring loosed the restraint he had been keeping on himself. He swung furiously on Pat.

"Why did you lie? What *is* the truth?"

The vehemence of the words and the gesture accompanying them told the blonde girl that she could only recapture his sympathy by a show of confession. Phil Morring was in a dangerous mood, a mood utterly foreign to her. She had to be cautious.

She did not want to lose him. He was an asset, as she viewed life. He had a good income, as she believed, and would be able to support a wife adequately, and she had always handled him easily.

She did not love him. She never had. But in the matter of her affection she made it a rule to be honest only with herself. In her code of social behaviour that was being smart, and smartness counted for a great deal with Patricia Laruce. The daughter of a chorus girl who had married a publican after burning her fingers with a scion of the aristocracy, she had imbibed her mother's warped outlook on life. Her sense of values was the product of a strange admixture of safety first and an insistent demand that life surrender to her those things that gave her pleasure. She played handmaid to opportunity. There was no need for opportunity to knock once. She was waiting with the door open.

"Jill," she said to the other girl, "I've a feeling that Phil is going to be unpleasant. Will you let us do our rag-picking alone?"

The dark-haired girl looked at Morring. She wanted to stay with a longing that surprised herself, but she said, "Of course, Pat. But don't be unkind—please."

Pat laughed.

"That's rich. I'm not about to put on a show. You'd better pass your request numbers on to Phil. He's taking the floor."

With a shrug Jill left it at that and went into the other room.

As the door closed Morring said, "I'm waiting to hear what you've got to say, Pat. I think you've been pretty despicable."

The make-up on her cheeks suddenly looked like daubs of colour on the face of a doll.

"And just why?" she asked, very calm.

"Those lies—dragging Jill into it—making me appear a fool, and—"

"Oh, that's where the shoe pinches, is it? Your pride's been chipped."

He eyed her steadily. "You made out to Slade that we weren't engaged—"

"For your sake. And this is what I get."

"My sake?"

"Of course. That detective was ready to build up a fine motive against you. He had the money. I didn't let him add me to it. You should be grateful."

He was disgusted. After what had taken place earlier her artifice was transparent.

"Can't you be honest with anyone?" he said bitterly. "You were thinking of yourself. That detective knows you went to Doyce's flat after the match, despite the way you made Jill back up your lie. And why did you go? Why was it so necessary?"

The only colour in her face now was artificial. She knew she had been brought to the edge of a crisis.

"Suppose you tell me. You seem to have developed a sudden vivid imagination."

"I'll tell you," he said, coming nearer. "You heard that the police were being called in. Doyce was dead. They would go to his flat and search the place, and there were things there you didn't want them to find, things that would require an explanation. I believe you deliberately broke your promise not to see Doyce again. I believe you and Doyce, both of you, thought I was a blind fool, and would never find out what was going on between you. I believe you went to his flat and brought away some of your personal things, because you had been his—"

"Stop!"

She was standing up. Emotion rode her like a storm. The crisis had broken. Foolishly she had thought she could avoid it, dance out of its swift path.

"All right, I loved John. But I wasn't deceitful. I intended telling you. I couldn't help falling for him. It was just luck—Fate—call it what you like."

"If I called it anything," he said coldly, "it would be a much less pleasant term."

She stood up to his contempt. She had to. She wasn't losing everything without a struggle. That was not her way. She was like her mother in that.

"I can't expect you to understand that I didn't want to cause you hurt, Phil. I can't expect you to realize that I was grateful for you and the times we had had, for what you had meant to me—"

"For God's sake stop play-acting!" He was weary, sick of the whole mess. His weariness crept into his voice. "You took my ring off when you thought it would serve you better that way—"

"That's not true!" she cried, fearful of what she saw in his face.

"You'd better leave it off," he finished relentlessly. "It'll suit me that way."

This brusque inversion of values stunned her. She was the one who could leave off his ring. She had done so when she pleased. His breaking with her—that was wrong. It wasn't what she wanted. She could throw him over if she wanted to; that was the game as she played it. He could not throw her over.

Panic swept her with the blinding force of a sirocco. She was being cut adrift. She was being turned down. The security to which she had clung was suddenly remote. She knew now that that was what Phil Morring had stood for in her life—security. Her mother had had a publican. She had found Phil Morring. And now—

The hysterical laugh that rose from her lips frightened her. She did not recognize it any more than she recognized the bewildering sensations sweeping through her mind, paralysing thought.

"You're jilting me. My God, that's too perfect! You sneered at John Doyce for playing fast and loose, and now you find the same game convenient. Just because you think the police will put their heads together and make me into a sweet little motive that might put a rope round your neck—"

The words were out, uttered with a trembling vindictiveness that appalled the man standing before her. She saw him shrink as though from a physical blow.

"You—you mean that!" he gasped.

She went on blindly, wanting to hurt him, to break what she mistakenly thought was his complacency.

"I don't have to," she said cruelly. "It was written all over those two detectives. They think you murdered John Doyce. They're trying to convict you. Even the papers are hinting at murder without actually putting the word into print. I'm the girl in the case now," she went on, spreading her hands in a defiant gesture.

"They know I lied about John, but I was smarter than you gave me credit for. I knew they'd think I was lying for your sake—"

"My sake!"

"Yes—yours. The same way they'd find out I lied about not being engaged to you. That would fit in neatly. All for your sake— they'd get there eventually. And why should I do it for your sake? Because, they would argue, I am really in love with you. It was my way of trying to protect you. And from there they'd get to the fact that you couldn't have murdered John Doyce—because with my loving you the way I had shown there was no cause— on my part. But you"—her voice rose, pitched to a trembling falsetto—"you throw me over. You can't trust me. You're not prepared to accept me as myself. You never loved me, or you couldn't doubt me so easily. You'd never throw me over just to protect yourself."

She stood back from him, eyes blazing. She had surprised her-self with this sudden sweeping attack, which had broken his new defence reared against her. Instinctively she had carried the battle forward at the crucial moment, when she thought everything lost.

He was staggered, bewildered, left utterly unsure of himself, of her, of anything.

"But, Pat—"

She pressed her advantage. She was one of those women who instinctively know how to handle men. Instinct was saving her now.

"No, Phil, it's too late. I'm not a toy. I'm glad you've shown me how little real faith you have in me."

The one thing she did not know—could not know—was that Phil Morring couldn't be trampled on, even by a conquering female. He had a pride that crushing merely stiffened.

"Then that settles everything, Pat. I'll be going."

She was momentarily at a loss to know how she had blundered. Had she overplayed her hand? She couldn't see how. The tactics she had employed had invariably been successful in her previous high-handed dealings with the other sex.

But now... In the very moment when she thought she had snatched victory out of defeat the tables were again turned on her. It didn't seem fair. It was against all the rules by which she played the complicated game of her life. She was near to tears when she said, "Then you've made up your mind—"

"No. I've to thank you for making it up for me."

"But—"

"You told me I never loved you. I think now you're right. I was infatuated, Pat. Your good looks, your high spirits, and the glamour you possess—they're what attracted me. Not *you*. Do you think anything could be the same after—*this?*"

Swiftly she summoned her last resources for a final despairing effort.

"You're hurt because I said I loved John Doyce. But I had to tell you the truth. Strangely, now that seems all far in the past. Only a few hours, yet years might have passed since yesterday. I—"

He was shaking his head.

"I'm not hurt because you loved Doyce instead of me. I'm just—enlightened. We made a great mistake, both of us. I'm prepared to admit it now."

The last effort had failed. Hot, searing anger that was near to hate filled her heart. But she kept this truth to herself. She must hold to dignity. She mustn't let him *see*. There would be a way of evening the count. But how remained her secret.

She said, "I always speed my parting lovers with a drink. What's yours, Phil?"

She could not understand why the colour left his face. He did not speak. He picked up his hat and went out without a last word.

She sat down, fists knotted. From a box on a side-table she took a cigarette and lit it. Jill came in.

"Phil gone?"

"This time for good. But he hasn't finished with me."

Her tone was a threat.

Jill crossed to her. "Pat, what are you saying? You don't mean—"

"Never mind what I mean." The blonde girl smoked quickly. "I can tell the police plenty that will interest them."

"You wouldn't be so mean!"

The alarm in the dark-haired girl's voice brought a bitter smile to the other's red mouth.

"You've always had a soft spot for Phil Morring, haven't you, Jill? You hated to think he wasn't properly appreciated—by yourself. How long have you been in love with him?"

Jill paled.

"You're—beastly!" she muttered.

"Because I can face the truth? Listen, darling, I've kept your secret a long while. Well, you're welcome to him. What's left when I'm through."

Jill fell back, as though struck.

"You wouldn't dare!" She was scared at this stranger she saw seated in front of her, this woman filled with hatred whose mouth was twisted in a sneer. "You couldn't go to the police with lies—"

"They won't be lies, pet. There was quite a quarrel not so long ago, and Phil Morring said some threatening words to his partner that couldn't possibly be misconstrued. Even such a soul of honour as yourself would have to tell the truth about that."

Pat rose, walked to the other door, which led to their bedroom.

"It looks as though everything's washed up. That suits me. Just remember that I can take care of myself. I always have, and I shall continue to. No man can wipe his feet on me and expect me to go on being the willing carpet."

Jill ran forward, caught the other girl's arm.

"Just a minute. You've had a lot to say. Before you leave there's something I want to tell you. I won't let you harm Phil. I stood by and saw you making a fool of him. And I said nothing—"

"Because you were scared, you sweet dumb-wit."

Jill ignored the gibe.

"You're utterly selfish. You've never thought of anyone except yourself—"

"Thanks for the charming reference."

"You're only thinking of yourself now."

"You're damned right I am."

"But you're making a big mistake if you think you're going to cause trouble for Phil now—"

"Still scared, eh? Want your precious hero untarnished. Well, I'm sorry to disappoint you. I'm going to pay him back in his own coin—and it's bad currency. And now for God's sake let go of my arm! I want to get dressed."

"Don't worry. I'm going out now, immediately. After this I want some clean air. I feel stifled. But I want you to know this. If you go to the police, pretending to tell the truth because you feel you must, I'll wreck your rotten scheme."

For some seconds they stood there by the door, acknowledged adversaries, with blades crossed.

"Go ahead, pet, try," mocked the blonde girl. "I've plenty to say that you know nothing about. I'm going to make that conceited fool damned sorry for giving me the run-around. I'm going to make him regret like hell that he ever thought himself too good for Pat Laruce."

The bedroom door slammed. She was gone.

Jill walked into the kitchen. The breakfast things and the coffee-cups were on the draining-board over the little sink. She dropped on to the plain wooden chair, and cried. She was utterly miserable. She felt helpless. She was crying half an hour later when the door into the hall landing shut loudly, and she was alone in the flat. Her grief was very personal, something that could not be shared.

It was true, she was in love with Phil Morring. Had been in love with him for long months while he had seen only Pat's blonde beauty and heard her laughter and empty promises. She had tried to resign herself to what she had considered the inevitable.

She thought she had succeeded. It had been hard, but she had disciplined herself. Her love was a thing never to be told.

Now it had been flung back at her by the woman who was determined to wreck Phil Morring's life out of petty spite and in revenge for the results of her own faithlessness. She had to find a way to save Phil. The police would believe Pat. She knew that.

He might even be arrested on a charge of murder. The thought numbed her mind. She could see the man she loved helpless against the force of circumstantial evidence. Little fragments of fact occurred to her.

That quarrel between Morring and his partner about Pat. The money, the ten thousand pounds for which they had been insured. Phil's trying to keep Doyce out of the Trojan team. The animosity between the two men that had grown strongly during recent weeks. Words. Accusations...

She could see how a clever detective might string all these pieces of fact together into a damning chain without an apparent weak link. Scraps she had read or heard in the past about innocent men being punished filtered into her clouded mind.

Phil was innocent!

The thought brought sharp pain. He was—he had to be!

It wasn't possible that he *had* murdered Doyce, hating him. Where could he have got the poison?

On the heels of the thought came an answer. Setchley might have provided a means.

She got to her feet, ignoring her stained, tear-wrecked face.

"Oh, God, it can't be true! No—it isn't!"

Resolutely she made the denial. She couldn't let him down now when he wanted some one's trust, when, as never before, he needed loyalty.

She suddenly knew she had to talk to him. She wanted to offer counsel, warn him. She must protect him as she now felt only she could.

Her love was a real thing. Her belief in him was a real thing...

She felt a little happier as she went into the sitting-room and picked up the telephone. She dialled the number of his flat and placed the receiver against her ear. She heard the making of contact, and then the purring of the receiver at the other end of the line.

But she did not hear Morring's voice.

At last she replaced the receiver and went slowly back to the kitchen. She turned on the hot-water tap and set about washing the cups and saucers and cutlery on the draining-board.

She felt very helpless and very alone.

IX

The Laboratory Report

THROUGHOUT THAT SUNDAY AFTER THE FATAL MATCH AT Highbury white-garbed men worked with frowning attention over their bunsens and retorts in the Home Office laboratory. The most modern batteries of the law in its war on crime were brought into action. Careful tests were made on the stomach organs of the dead man.

Alkaloid poisoning of some kind was proved. Reagents provided an answer that left no doubt. Doyce had been murdered.

While special tests to isolate the particular poison were begun the news was handed out to the Press.

On Monday morning all Britain knew that the Yard was seeking a murderer.

"All I hope is, Slade finds him quick," said Ted Drake, swinging at a punch-ball in the Arsenal gym.

Bryn Jones, his face moist, paused in his pull at the rowing machine.

"Here's Chulley," he said, "the Trojan skipper. Maybe he's got an idea."

He rose, wiped his forehead on the sleeve of his maroon training jersey. Chulley looked glum. He was talking to the Arsenal coach, Jack Lambert.

"How do you fellows feel about this?" asked Drake, leaving the punch-ball.

Chulley shrugged.

"I don't know. The boys don't feel much like talking. You know how it is."

"According to the papers this morning there's no doubt about it being murder." Bryn Jones's Celtic features looked troubled. "It takes some getting used to."

"But who—" began Drake, and stopped suddenly.

Chulley jerked his head. "That's all right, Ted. You don't have to think of my feelings. I know what you must be thinking, all of you. One of us did it." His fists knotted. "I'd like to know who," he muttered. "This is going to hit the old man hard. He's taken some bad knocks while getting the Trojans together, and now—"

There was an awkward pause, filled in by Drake, who turned to Lambert.

"You played against the Saxon Rovers, Jack. Ever turn out against Doyce or that red-haired winger Setchley?"

Lambert shook his head.

"They were after my time. But look here, you haven't finished—"

He was interrupted when a bounding ball smote his legs.

"Hey!" yelled Swindin, at the farther end of the gym.

Lambert booted the ball back towards the goalkeeper. Drake flogged the punch-ball, making it sing. He stepped away from it.

"I'm going down," he said. "Untie these, Jack."

Lambert untied the laces of his boxing-gloves.

"Coming, Bryn? You, Chulley?"

The three players pushed through the swing-door. Lambert watched them go, said nothing. He knew that Arsenal men and

Trojans alike that morning were "nervy." It was a new sensation for the normally happy, boisterous players to work under the eye of the police, as though they were criminals.

Slade and Clinton had arrived some while before, were at that moment with Allison in the manager's room. The players were going through their routine training day, trying to appear as though nothing unusual had happened. But occasionally a man's curiosity got the better of him. He wanted to know what the others thought and felt.

Lambert walked up to the other end of the gym.

"Come on, up to it, lad. That's the way," he encouraged a youngster of the Enfield nursery club, which he managed.

A group of youngsters in grey sweaters and navy shorts were practising heading a ball. Swindin was saving the shots, fisting the ball against the wire screens protecting windows and ceiling lights. The juniors were less perturbed by the occasion than the older men.

On the training ground behind the south terrace Eddie Hapgood was playing his usual vigorous game of head tennis. The game closed with a shout. The players paused to mop their faces.

"What do you think, Eddie?" asked Male.

There was no need to say what about.

The grin on the Arsenal captain's face was replaced by a look of frank puzzlement.

"I'm not a detective, George. But it looks bad for the Trojans." Hapgood glanced to where the bulk of the Trojan team were practising with a ball at the other end of the training-ground. "I had a word with Raille this morning when he arrived. He didn't want to talk, and it's understandable, after all."

"Sure, with Kindilett an old Saxon Rovers director," said Male.

"What's that got to do with it?" asked Crayston, who had overheard the remarks.

"Doyce had only been in the team a little over a week. Must be bad blood somewhere."

"That doesn't follow," contended Hapgood sharply. "There have been plenty of rumours about us, if it comes to that. Specially when we struck a bad patch. But it meant nothing. Talk about bad blood in a team usually does mean nothing. You should know that, George."

"I didn't mean it that way," said Male. "I meant bad blood outside the team, but on the part of the players."

"I don't get it," said Crayston.

"Doyce had a business partner, who is in the team," Male pointed out. "There could have been something in their private life, couldn't there?"

This was received in silence.

"Suppose there was a girl—" muttered Crayston.

"Cut it," snapped Hapgood. "Let's join the others. Hallo! Here come Chulley and those we left in the gym."

Lithe as a cat in his grey suede training-suit, the Arsenal captain bounded away. The others followed.

"Raille out here?" called Chulley.

"No, he's upstairs with the boss," shouted Hapgood above the hubbub of voices. "Here—hold it!"

He sent a hard cross-drive at the Trojan captain, who trapped the ball neatly and smacked it straight at Male. The Londoner heeled it towards Crayston, and the half back promptly got his head to it and tried to take Hapgood off-guard.

Meantime the Trojan trainer was facing Slade in Allison's room. Allison and Clinton stood to one side of the desk. Kindilett sat by the door.

"I believe you called at Doyce's flat Friday evening," Slade was saying. "Did he have any visitors, Raille?"

"Why, not that I know of."

Raille looked as though he wanted to ask a question, but didn't like to.

"That the first time you'd been?" asked Slade.

"No. I'd been there before. Last Tuesday I think it was. I wanted to make sure Doyce was in shape for Saturday."

"Was he?"

"I think so. He seemed in good spirits, anyway."

"When, Tuesday or Friday?"

"Both days."

"There's one thing I want to know," Slade continued, "and I'd like you to think carefully before replying, Raille. Were Morring and Doyce friendly in the dressing-room?"

Raille moved his feet. He looked uncomfortable.

"I did think they kept apart, but"—he shrugged—"it wasn't noticeable."

"Yet you noticed it."

"Well, I suppose I did. But I don't think anyone else would have done so."

Slade didn't press him to explain in more detail. "Were they together at half-time?" was his next question.

"I can't say. I gave Doyce his package, then talked to them altogether. I don't know if those two spoke. We hadn't much time, you know."

"Did you see what Doyce took from his package?"

"No."

"Another thing, Raille. The rest of the team must feel deeply about what's happened. Have they talked? You, as trainer, would hear anything they had to say."

Raille dropped his gaze. "They haven't said much."

Slade leaned forward. "I want you to get out of your head, Raille, any idea that you're tittle-tattling by answering my questions frankly. A man has been murdered. That's bad for the team. It means a murderer has to be found. It's up to you to help in any way you can."

The trainer stood silent.

"Even if it means the arrest of one of the team," added Slade, as though reading the man's thoughts.

After several more seconds Raille glanced up.

"Doyce wasn't liked," he said slowly. "His manner was cocksure, and it didn't go down with the others. He was a newcomer, and he hadn't any tact. Perhaps he was over-confident—"

"Raille," said the Yard man as the trainer hesitated, "did Doyce quarrel with any of the team?"

"That I can't say."

"Can't?"

"I mean because I don't know."

"I see." Slade studied some notes he had spread out before him. "You say Doyce was cocksure. I have reason to believe he was popular with the other sex. Know anything about that?"

Raille shook his head.

"Yet you visited his flat."

"That's true, I did—twice. I'm afraid I don't understand, Inspector."

"Mean you didn't see the photos of his lady friends?"

"No."

Slade stood up. "All right, Raille, that'll be all for now, thank you."

The trainer, after a glance at the unhappy Kindilett, went out, closing the door.

Allison moved away from the wall.

"You didn't get much from him," the Arsenal manager reflected.

"No," said Slade, "I didn't. I think Raille mistrusts the publicity his team are getting."

"Surely that's natural," said Kindilett, his voice flat.

"Natural. But my job isn't to study people's feelings," Slade pointed out.

"Then you think he was holding something back?" queried Kindilett.

"I can't tell. He wasn't very communicative about Doyce—"

The 'phone rang. Slade picked up the receiver, listened, and said, "Put them through, please."

Half a minute later he pursed his mouth.

"Aconitine. Yes—yes, I get that. Right. Oh, about an hour or so. Yes, I want that report."

He sat back and dropped the receiver in its cradle.

"Well," he told his audience, "we now know which poison killed Doyce. Aconitine. It's one of the most deadly poisons known. The lab. has just reported."

Kindilett shook his head sadly.

"All this is more distressing than I can say. I have been hoping that there has been some—some blunder. That Doyce wasn't—" He broke off, added heavily, "But he was."

His head sank on his chest.

Allison glanced meaningly at Slade.

"I'd like to see them at work on the training-ground," said the detective.

"All right, I'll take you down, Inspector." Allison turned to Kindilett. "You stay here, Francis. Have a drink. You know where it is."

The two Yard men and the Arsenal manager went out, leaving Kindilett in his attitude of dejection.

"He's taking it hard," grunted Allison.

Neither Slade nor Clinton offered any comment. They followed Allison down the corridor along which the players filed on to the ground, walked to the end of the East Stand and passed by the first-aid room, and came round to the training-ground. Steel netting enclosed the ground on two sides. Allison led the way through an iron gate on to the red-surfaced ground.

About thirty players were divided into two groups, each dribbling and shooting before a goal. The balls smacked against boots and goal-posts, performed crazy geometric designs in the air.

"An hour at this is hard work," Allison explained to the Yard men.

"I can believe it," said Slade.

"The game to-day is faster than it's ever been," the Arsenal manager added. "Only the fit can survive."

"And hope to win the League Championship," put in Clinton.

Allison smiled.

"Hey! Look out!"

The sudden shout sent all three looking in the direction from which it came. A swiftly travelling ball had cannoned from Hapgood's foot. Setchley, his back towards the Arsenal captain, stood in its path. At the shout the Trojan player turned to see what was the matter. Before he could jump clear or throw up his arms the ball had struck him on the left side of his chest.

With a short cry he fell over.

"He's hurt," said Allison, running forward.

The two Yard men moved with him. But before they could reach the fallen player Raille was bending over him. Setchley was clasping his chest and moaning through tight lips.

"Better get him inside," Allison advised. "Tom will give you something to fix him, Raille."

Supported by the Trojan trainer, Setchley hobbled off the training-ground.

"Perhaps we'd better follow," Slade suggested. "I don't think it was the ball that hurt him."

"Hapgood's got a hefty kick," said Allison.

"All the same, I'm curious," said the Yard man.

They left the training-ground and returned to the Stadium. In the Arsenal dressing-room Whittaker was already examining Setchley's chest. The injured player was on a treatment table.

"Nasty bruise," said Whittaker, looking closely at the discoloured skin under his fingers. "Hurt much?"

"Bit," said Setchley, grinning with an effort.

"It's not a fresh place," Whittaker decided.

"No, he's had it about a week," Raille informed his fellow-trainer. "It's been all right, but I suppose that bang just now has made it sore."

"Sore's the word, Raille." Setchley propped himself up on his elbows as Whittaker began dabbing with iodine. "Good job it didn't happen Saturday."

There was no comment on this.

"That ought to fix you," said Whittaker, drawing back and surveying his handiwork. "It'll come up dark after a few hours, but it shouldn't trouble you too much."

"How did you get the bruise?" asked Slade casually.

Setchley looked at the Yard man, grinned. "Not playing soccer, as you might imagine."

"Thought it wasn't the result of a smack with a ball," Whittaker nodded, wiping his stained fingers on a towel. "Banged yourself against something sharp, didn't you?"

"Yes. Of all things, against the bench in my lab.," admitted the red-haired Trojan ruefully. "Week ago—yes, last Monday. Nasty knock. I was reaching over to take some papers from Morring and my foot slipped."

"From Morring?" Slade echoed.

Setchley nodded, pulled down his practice shirt, and jumped off the table.

"That's right. He'd been lecturing me some time about taking out an insurance policy. Well, he'd finally got me to the acquiescent stage. I said I'd look over his suggestions, and he took me at my word. Came out to the lab. and made me sign on the dotted line."

"Where is your lab.?"

"Great West Road. Small place, but we get through quite a bit of work."

"All research work?"

"Mostly." Setchley looked up suddenly, aware that the detective's questions were no longer casual. "Experimental, certainly," he added guardedly.

"Must be interesting," Slade mused. "Keep any aconitine handy?"

"Of course. Matter of fact—" The red-headed man caught his breath, and his greeny-blue eyes lit with sharpened interest. "So that was it—aconitine. Alkaloid. Explains a lot."

"I hope it'll explain everything," said Slade dryly, following the trend of the other's thoughts. "In due course."

Setchley ran his hands over his head.

"Nice work isolating it so soon," he said appreciatively. "Can never tell with the alkaloids. Might waste a lot of time if one—"

Again he stopped short. A worried look crossed his face.

"Come to think of it, doesn't look too good for me, does it?" he challenged Slade.

"A coincidence is rarely conclusive," Slade smiled.

Setchley's head jerked. "Nice to hear you say so, Inspector. But just for the minute—"

He shuddered dramatically.

"You were going to say something about aconitine a few moments ago," Slade reminded him. "You said, 'matter of fact,' and stopped. Remember?"

Setchley pinched his nose between finger and thumb.

"That's right. When you mentioned the stuff. I was going to say that six months ago we were using aconitine in the lab. We were experimenting with heart stimulants. Aconitine and the antidote digitalin. Interesting—on paper." He glanced at Slade. "You don't need me to tell you it's pretty fierce stuff."

"So I've gathered," Slade nodded. "What's the record?"

He was watching the Trojan player closely, but Setchley now seemed unperturbed, interested only in an academic problem.

"One-sixteenth of a grain has been known to prove lethal," he reflected. "A man has died within eight minutes of it entering his bloodstream. That would depend upon his condition."

"Doyce was fit."

Setchley's lips compressed. "Yes, there would be more resistance. But he was exercising. His circulation was speeded up. That would tend to accelerate the action."

"So that it would be sudden?"

"Certainly." Setchley took a deep breath. "Now, if you don't mind, Inspector, I'll get under the shower."

"Of course. Thanks for the information."

Followed by Allison and Clinton, Slade left the dressing-room.

"That must be coincidence," Allison said, rattling loose change in a trousers pocket.

"We'll see," returned Slade non-committally. "I want those seals kept on the treatment room door, Mr Allison, and—er—I've got your tie-pin in my case."

Allison smiled wryly. "Your people found no aconitine on *that*."

"Nor on any of the other pins we took on Saturday. I've brought them all back. By the way, Mr Allison, if you don't mind my saying so, that's a rather unique pin of yours. A double pearl shaped like a death's head."

"I've had it some years now," Allison explained. "It's a kind of mascot. Certainly I've never seen another like it. As you say, it's a double pearl shaped like a death's head. The eyes are ruby chips, and the nose is a sapphire, and the mouth is a diamond chip. It has a unique history, too, beginning with King Ferdinand of Bulgaria. I was thinking Saturday night that it was a rather grim emblem, in the circumstances," he added ruefully.

Conversation became more general, and not long afterwards Slade and Clinton left the Stadium. As they drove back to the Yard Clinton said, "Well, we've got somewhere at last. Setchley with the actual stuff on tap, and proof that Morring had a chance to get it. I didn't think it would pan out as easily as this."

Slade shook his head.

"Clinton," he said, "it's beginning to look too good to be true."

"I don't see why. This isn't a clever murder."

"I'm not so sure. We haven't found the weapon yet," Slade reminded him. "Anyway, what I meant was everything's turning out too pat in the case against Morring."

"You've got three pointers," Clinton ruminated. "The money, the girl—who's a liar and looks it—and now the poison. There's a case in that much."

"All the same, let's hear the report on that cutting. I was told on the 'phone that one's come through."

The report was on Slade's desk when they arrived at the Yard. It was from the police at Ryechester. They had traced the cutting from a copy of the *Ryechester Chronicle* of four years before. The word "fosse" had given them the needed clue. Attached to the report was a summary of a coroner's inquest, the subject of the cutting.

"Good God!" breathed Clinton, reading over Slade's shoulder. "Kindilett's daughter! Found drowned after going to a dance. Verdict of death by misadventure."

Slade dropped the report on to his desk.

"This certainly alters things," he agreed gravely.

"It doesn't alter anything," Clinton maintained stoutly. "Ryechester—Kindilett—the Saxon Rovers. It all ties in neat as a sailor's knot. Morring again. He was in the Rovers four years ago. He must have known all about that case down in Ryechester. He—This is what copper-bottoms the case against him."

Although he didn't admit it to the sergeant, Slade felt suddenly depressed. The case against Morring, as he saw it, was suspiciously complete. It could hardly be more conclusive if it had been specially prepared to implicate the dead man's partner. Stage by stage it had grown, in a strangely natural sequence, each additional discovery the result of routine investigation.

Further, Morring's own actions had done nothing to lessen suspicion. True, he had come forward with a story, but not a complete story. He had acted with suspicion on Sunday, suddenly leaving the golf club-house and driving to London. Followed, Slade had been presented by a suspect plainly angry with a girl who claimed she was not engaged to him. To-day Morring had kept clear of the Yard men. Slade had seen him on the training-ground. But he had not rushed up to Setchley when the old Saxon Rover had fallen.

Morring had certainly not helped himself by his actions. He was the number one logical suspect, and the evidence was piling up logically against him.

"Another thing," Clinton went on, cutting across Slade's reflection, "he's the only one who fits every condition. It's always been your contention in the past that that's a fair test of the case against any suspect."

"You think we should arrest him, Clinton?"

"I think we ought to give him another going-over. With what we've got to play with he might crack, and we'd finish the case with a confession. It wouldn't surprise me."

Slade lit his pipe, considered the sergeant's words.

"There's a lot to be said for your argument, Clinton, but"—he shook his head—"somehow I'm not convinced. Not utterly. I've a feeling that this crime was cleverly planned. It is full of interesting psychological factors—the cutting, the package, the time, the setting—I'm certain all these have a human value, if we could find it. I think the murderer has used considerable foresight. More, I think he has been too clever to be trapped by simple progressive developments—"

"Simple!" Clinton scouted the idea.

"Nevertheless, considered in sequence, that case against Morring is *simple.*"

Clinton frowned at his chief. He had been following Slade's reasoning, and he knew there was a great deal in what Slade said.

"You think Morring is being framed—cleverly framed?"

Slade sat down.

"That's the devil of it, I can't tell. I can't even begin to satisfy myself. It may all be circumstance—"

"Coincidence!" Clinton scoffed.

"If you prefer," Slade said, undeterred. "But the possibility must be considered—"

"Don't forget the possibility of guilt," grunted the sergeant, still persistent.

Slade cleared his lungs of smoke. "Tell you what, Clinton," he said. "We'll run down to Ryechester and see just what goes to this angle—this death by misadventure of Kindilett's daughter Mary. It may throw some light on the whole problem."

"It's certainly an angle we must cover. That cutting was intended to mean something."

"Yes—to Doyce."

At this stage they were interrupted by a rap on the door. A uniformed constable looked in.

"Miss Patricia Laruce to see you, Inspector," he announced.

Slade glanced at Clinton. "Maybe our yeast did work, after all," he commented dryly.

"Show her in," he told the constable.

X

Out of the Past

THE BLONDE GIRL TOOK THE SEAT SLADE PLACED FOR HER, crossed her legs, and patted the end of her dress. She held up a newspaper.

"I bought this half an hour ago," she told them. "It says the poison that killed John Doyce was aconitine."

"That's quite right. You have something to tell us about it?" Slade inquired.

"I've decided I had better be frank with you," she said. "Put my cards on the table."

"An excellent idea," Slade commended. "But what has made you change your mind?"

"I haven't changed my mind," she said quickly. "I was quite willing to help you yesterday, but you made things very awkward for me, in front of Phil and Miss Howard."

"I'm sorry."

Slade shot a glance at Clinton. The sergeant was hiding a grin in a large hand.

"But now it's different," she went on. "I realized I could talk more freely here, and—well, the truth is I don't want to get mixed up in a murder case. I've got myself to think of, haven't I?"

"Of course," Slade murmured. "What do you want to tell me?"

"First, I was at John Doyce's flat on Saturday. I'm afraid I deceived you about that. But Phil's temper is something I fear. I just couldn't admit to it in front of him. I went to the flat to get some things. Silly of me, but I did. You see, I'd fallen in love with John, and he—well, we felt the same way about each other. Phil wouldn't understand. As he saw it we were engaged—"

"You told me you weren't engaged," Slade pointed out.

"I'm afraid that was another little deceit," she said easily, trying to brush aside the interruption. "I had to be careful in front of Phil. He had already quarrelled with John about me, threatened that if he saw me again—I mean—Oh, it was all so beastly, so awful!"

She broke off, giving a fair presentation of injured and misunderstood innocence.

"You suddenly decided to tell me this?" Slade prompted.

"That's right. I was tired of being misunderstood."

Slade's brows lifted. "I can assure you there's no danger of that here, Miss Laruce."

She gave him a straight look. "Thank you. I knew I was doing right in coming here. I'm no longer engaged to Phil Morring, and I feel I have no reason now for—for trying to camouflage anything. You do understand, don't you?"

"Not entirely," Slade admitted. "The engagement was broken off—when?"

"Sunday, after you left."

Slade risked another glance at Clinton. The sergeant was now grinning behind two hands.

"I see. You were in love with Doyce, and you were going to tell Morring—"

"But naturally," she whispered, in feigned surprise that he should even mention the matter.

"But you were afraid of his temper?"

"Yes, that's it—his temper. That's just it. I see you do understand."

"One other thing, Miss Laruce," said Slade. "Do you know if Morring visited Setchley at the latter's laboratory?"

"Well, Phil didn't tell me himself, but I remember John told me Setchley was taking out a policy with the firm and Phil had been out to see him to fix things. Early last week, I think it was."

She cast wide, innocent, baby eyes round the room.

"Why, is that helpful?" she asked.

"It may be," Slade nodded. "Can you tell me more about the quarrel between Morring and Doyce?"

"I can, but I'd rather not," she said, dropping her gaze.

"I'm afraid we'll have to know, Miss Laruce. It may be important."

"But I assure you it isn't—really."

Slade held up a hand, prepared to play the scene through as she wished.

"You must allow me to judge that."

With well-simulated dejection she described a quarrel that almost came to blows between the two men. She contrived to give the impression that she was merely an innocent bystander at the time, afraid of what would happen. But she made it very clear that Morring had been in a towering rage and had threatened physical injury to Doyce if a similar incident occurred.

Slade took her up immediately.

"Morring knew you were visiting Doyce's flat again?"

She strove to look indignant at the hidden implication, but Slade wasn't impressed, and she desisted.

"He may have done. I don't know." Her tone was now sullen. The interview had not gone quite as she had planned, yet she could not discover where or how she had made a mistake. "I've told you all I know."

She rose.

"Well, it was very good of you, Miss Laruce, to take so much trouble."

"I felt I had to let you know the whole truth," she murmured, with an angelic smile.

"If we want you we can get you at the same address?" Slade said.

She frowned, tapped the side of her mouth with a gloved finger.

"Well, no. I've left. I found it impossible to stay under the same roof as Miss Howard after Sunday. But you can get me at Commer-Photos. I'm staying with a friend to-day and to-morrow, and hoping to get a place for myself on Wednesday. Good morning."

The door closed after her.

Clinton dropped his hands. "Nice girl," he muttered, with heavy sarcasm. "Just walks in to tell us the whole truth and slip a noose round her fiancé's neck. I know what I'd like to do with her, the double-crossing little—"

"Sh! You should be happy, Clinton, to find another piece that fits into the case against Morring. A threat now. Shows premeditation, something this crime needs. How about it?"

Clinton pulled a wry face. "I'd like to get Morring off just to cheat that little peroxided schemer," he said savagely. "If there's one type of woman I can't stand—"

"Don't bother about one," Slade grinned. "I know several already, including our little photographer's model. Seems we broke up the happy home on Sunday. It's Morring's turn now to come out with something." Slade became serious. "He'll have to be quick about it if he's going to do himself any good," he added thoughtfully.

Clinton was already studying a Bradshaw.

"There's a train to Ryechester in forty minutes. We've got time to get something to eat and catch it."

They arrived at the Ryechester police station in the middle of the afternoon. Inspector Dunning, a grey-haired veteran of the local force, was expecting them.

"The *Chronicle* people may be able to give you some extra details," he told them. "We haven't got the Rovers any more, as you know, and of course that Kindilett affair is forgotten. Four years can be a long time."

"You remember the case yourself, Dunning?" Slade asked.

"Only vaguely. I was away up North at the time, and heard about it when I got back. I know there was some sort of scandal."

"What sort?"

"Well, talk mostly. Old women's gossip. The verdict at the inquest was death by misadventure, as you saw in the report we sent. But I remember there was a lot of vague hinting at suicide. There had been an unfortunate love affair, which was rather kept in the background. Kindilett had friends, you know, and they rallied round. There wasn't a lot brought out that could have been."

"Then she might have committed suicide?"

The local man shrugged. "She was found in the fosse. No one could say she *didn't* throw herself in. No one came forward to say she *did*. It's like that. Take your choice. But, if you don't mind my asking, what's all this got to do with your business last Saturday?"

Slade told Dunning. The local man listened with close attention. When Slade had finished he sat back, his hands clasped.

"I don't know that you'll get a great deal of help down here, Slade," he said doubtfully. "Kindilett himself is your best source of information—if he'll talk."

"Exactly," the Yard man nodded. "If the inquest was soft-pedalled, he certainly won't want to drag up all that past history again. It wouldn't be pleasant."

"True enough," Dunning agreed. "He tore up his roots when he left these parts. But he was a father for whom the sun rose and set on his daughter. There was a great deal of sympathy for him at the time. But we've nothing in the files here that can help you. Nothing at all."

The two Yard men called at the offices of the *Ryechester Chronicle*, a green-painted shop with a window full of local pictures with typed legends. A desultory youth who seemingly had great difficulty in controlling a mop of flaxen hair looked up at their entry. He had been reading a boy's weekly, well crumpled and fingered.

"Mr Fingleton?" he queried sharply.

"Who's he?" asked Slade.

The boy sat up, took more interest in his visitors.

"'Vertisement manager."

"We want to see the editor."

"Got an appointment? Mr Clarke's busy. He's always busy," he added diplomatically.

But diplomacy was lost in a rush of boyish awe when Slade gave him his official card and asked him to take it to Mr Clarke.

"Gee!"

He was away from the counter and gone through a glass-panelled door with the word.

"You'll be lucky if they don't insert it in the small ads," Clinton suggested.

Slade chose to ignore the sally. After an interval of nearly three minutes the fair-haired boy returned.

"Mr Clarke'll see you. This way, please."

They passed round the counter, went through the glass-panelled door, and twisted themselves in and out of corded bundles of the *Ryechester Chronicle*. The boy hopped ahead and seized hold of the handle of another door, on which the word "Editor" was all but worn away.

He threw open the door with the air of a victor tossing away a laurel wreath.

"Inspector Slade of Scotland Yard," he announced, his young voice vibrant with strange personal triumph.

Slade and Clinton saw a shirt-sleeved young man of about twenty-five get out of an old chair set before an older roll-top desk piled with galley slips and sheets of typing.

"I thought that young rip was pulling another of his confounded jokes," said the young man, who exuded an air of tired efficiency. "I'm Clarke, the editor. I hope there hasn't been any trouble, gentlemen."

He looked a trifle nervous. Slade, surprised to find so young a man in charge of even a small local paper, sat down in the chair pushed forward for him.

"I came wanting information about something that happened here four years ago, Mr Clarke."

"I know. Inspector Dunning got on to Mr Hakers. He's the proprietor of the *Chronicle*, and—well, he controls the policy and keeps a tight hand on things."

Clarke smiled, and Slade, who realized now why the young man had the job and what was expected of him, smiled back in sympathy. It wasn't the first time Slade had sought information in the offices of a small local newspaper.

"I want a copy of the edition carrying the story of the inquest," said the detective.

Clarke nodded.

"I can manage that. Anything else?"

"Photos? They might help if you have any."

"Sure. I'll see what I can do."

He left the two Yard men and went out. Nearly ten minutes passed before he came back. He had a newspaper and an illustration "original" that had been touched up with Chinese white. The paper carried the story of the inquest on an inside page, and the story ran to nearly two columns, including a verbatim report on Kindilett's evidence. Doyce and Setchley also gave evidence.

Slade ran his eye down the columns, saw that they would provide him with quite an amount of detail, and glanced at the illustration at the top of the page. It showed a group of football players in hooped shirts and dark knickers. At one side of the group was a girl. At the other side was a man in ordinary clothes. The latter had a moustache.

"This is the photo we made the block from. I thought it would be clearer," added Clarke.

"Thanks," Slade said gratefully.

On the back was pencilled, "Some of the Saxon Rovers. Mary Kindilett at left-hand of group." It said nothing about the man with the moustache. But at the bottom was a rubber-stamped address, "Peter Prines, 10 Crayle Street, Ryechester."

Slade pointed to the address.

"This man Prines. He still here?"

Clarke nodded. "Very much so. Doesn't touch Press stuff any more. He's come up in the world. Portraits at fancy figures. Big do's occasionally. But he knows his stuff. Good cameraman."

"Many thanks. I don't think we need detain you any longer, Mr Clarke. I'd like to keep this copy and the photo—"

"Sure. That's all right. Only"—the young editor hesitated—"if you can let me have something—early," he stressed, "I'd be grateful. I know you're busy and—"

"I'll drop a word to Dunning. He'll probably help you out."

"That's very nice of you, Inspector. I'd like to get a local slant on this case. The nationals are giving it a big boost."

They left him preparing to wrestle again with the pile of papers on the roll-top desk. In the outer office the boy looked up from his twopenny thriller. He followed them with eloquent eyes.

In the street again, Slade said, "We're getting somewhere at last."

He sounded pleased.

The sergeant gave him a side-glance. He knew that tone in his superior's voice. It usually indicated that Slade was finding things working out.

"Can't see it myself. I'm hoping this Prines fellow will give us some help."

As it turned out, Peter Prines evinced a ready inclination to be of whatever service he could. He was a short man, tubby, thin on top, with a pair of eloquent hands. They were always moving, always giving queer emphasis to his words.

He studied the picture Slade gave him, listened carefully to the detective's explanation of how he had come by it, and nodded his head in a quick, bird-like fashion.

"M'm, m'm, I remember," he nodded. "I was doing quite a bit of leg-work for the locals."

Slade glanced at the well-tailored black jacket with the red carnation in the buttonhole, at the knife-edge crease in the grey-striped trousers falling over well-polished willow-calf shoes. Mr Peter Prines had come a long way from his leg-work for local newspapers, unless appearances lied very considerably.

"Sad case that Mary Kindilett business," he murmured, shaking his head. "Her father was liked by everyone. Sad business indeed."

"You remember the inquest?"

"Distinctly. There was quite a commotion when her fiancée didn't come forward."

"Oh." Slade looked interested. "How was that?"

"Well, she'd been engaged, but had broken it off about two or three days before she was found drowned, if I remember rightly. I recall her father stated that he didn't know the name of the man. For myself, I'm pretty sure I know why he didn't come forward."

"You are?"

"Supposing he had," said Mr Prines, looking sorrowful, "what would have happened? There would have been a lot of discussion and questions back-firing, and ten to one the jury would have decided she had chucked herself in the fosse—suicide. See? That would have been a reflection on her. It—well, it wouldn't have been nice, would it?"

Slade agreed that it wouldn't. Mr Prines continued.

"As it was, he didn't come forward. There were all sorts of rumours, but without anyone to pin them to, what could they do?" He appealed to the detectives. They waited for the answer they knew he would supply. "They brought in a verdict of death by misadventure. See? An accident. My opinion is her fiancé stayed away from court on purpose to save her father suffering."

"She went to a dance on the night of the misadventure," said Slade.

"True. I remember now. And it was one of those footballers took her. Wait a minute, his name's on the tip of my tongue. I can see him now, standing up giving evidence, a dark-haired fellow, very sure of himself, nattily dressed, and—Good God!" Mr Prines bounced on the balls of his feet. "John Doyce! It was him. So that's why you're down here!"

He was suddenly animated. Arms and legs moved, fingers flexing, knees crooking, as though he couldn't keep still. His eyes danced.

"What a fool not to think of it! Of course!" he exclaimed. "Kindilett—Doyce dead—that dance. Pity, pity!" He shook his head, suddenly to change the motion to a nod. "A great pity indeed."

"For whom?" Slade inquired mildly.

Mr Prines looked surprised.

"Why, for Francis Kindilett! The whole thing will be dished up again, hot and steaming in the dailies, now Scotland Yard are down here clue-hunting. His daughter, and now the man who took her to that dance. What a story!"

"I suppose you don't happen to know, yourself, who was Mary Kindilett's fiancé?" said Slade hopefully.

"I don't." It seemed he put an unnecessary emphasis on the denial. "I don't know anyone who does. It was a complete mystery."

"Have the Kindilett family any relatives left in the town?"

"I don't think so. I never heard of any. The mother died a good many years ago, I believe. No, when Kindilett moved I think the last of them went."

Mr Prines was quite prepared to go on talking as long as they would listen, but Slade drew the interview to a close with a word of thanks. The photographer bowed them out of his studio. The

Yard men called back at the police station, where Slade had a few minutes' talk with Dunning, and then they hurried to catch a train to London.

Both were silent. Clinton was frankly puzzled how to fit in the new details with the case as he saw it—which was one against Morring. He did venture a half-hearted suggestion.

"Suppose Morring were the missing fiancé."

But Slade scouted the idea.

"You've built your case against him, Clinton, on how he's reacted in a similar situation—a girl and Doyce. Wouldn't he have done the same then? You're allowing a bad inconsistency."

Clinton was compelled to reconsider his theory. Slade's objection was strong and logical. If Morring had been Mary Kindilett's fiancé, and the engagement had been broken off, presumably on account of Doyce, then surely he would have reacted just as positively as he had when Doyce had robbed him of Patricia Laruce. By such reasoning, Doyce would have been found dead, not Mary Kindilett.

Yet without admitting Morring as the fiancé of Mary Kindilett, how explain the cutting found in Doyce's clothes?

That had been a personal reminder of this tragedy of four years ago. A reminder presumably with a bearing on what was happening recently. It was a piece of the puzzle which fitted—but where—how?

If Morring wasn't the girl's fiancé, then Clinton's whole case was weakened. He would have to admit another fiancé, another person with a strong reason to hate Doyce.

Or would he?

"Let me see the account of the inquest," he said.

Slade passed over the copy of the *Ryechester Chronicle*. Clinton read through Doyce's evidence. Yes, he had taken the girl to the dance, but admitted that she had disappeared some time before the end. He had searched for her, but had not been able to find her. He had 'phoned her home, but got no reply. He had not quarrelled with her, he claimed. They were good friends. He did not know the name of her fiancé. He had thought her engagement a joke. He was hurt and surprised when he heard her body had been found.

That was all. The usual line such a witness might be expected to take, admitting little.

Clinton gave the paper back to Slade.

"Thought of something?" asked the latter.

The sergeant nodded moodily.

"Plenty, but it doesn't make sense. I think, from that account, Doyce was playing the same game as every one else. Holding back information."

"To protect a dead girl's name," Slade mused.

"Maybe," Clinton grunted. "Or maybe to protect himself. It doesn't look so good for him. He took her to the dance, he was catching her on the rebound after breaking off the engagement, probably caused her to break it off. We know he was good at fixing engagements—"

"Didn't he say he thought the whole thing a joke?"

"That was clever of him. Threw a wrench in the works right away. Made his opinion not worth asking, and so let him off lightly."

"Clinton," said Slade, "you're a cynic."

That closed the discussion, each man returning to his private meditation.

It was dusk when they entered London. They drove from the station to the Yard, and in the office of Department X2 found a memorandum awaiting them.

Setchley had 'phoned the Yard earlier that afternoon, and had left a message for Inspector Slade. The message was marked "Urgent." Setchley was reporting that the bottle of aconitine usually kept in the poison cabinet of his laboratory was missing. Neither he nor his assistant, Tompkins, knew when it had disappeared or whence.

He and his assistant would be at the laboratory until seven o'clock, in case they were wanted.

XI

Who Stole the Poison?

SETCHLEY WAS ON THE POINT OF LEAVING WHEN SLADE AND Clinton arrived at the laboratory in the Great West Road. Like most research laboratories, this one was housed in an insignificant and rather dilapidated building. It was tucked away between two large factories with imposing concrete façades.

"I thought you weren't coming," said the red-haired chemist.

"We've only just got back from Ryechester," Slade explained, and watched the other, to see how he took the news.

He made no attempt to conceal his surprise.

"Ryechester? But what were you doing down there, Inspector? Getting old Saxon Rovers' background?"

"Among other things. I wanted to find out what was said at Mary Kindilett's inquest."

Mention of the girl's name affected the chemist strangely. He started, opened his mouth to speak, but apparently thought better of it. He showed them into a small cubby-hole at the end of a narrow corridor.

"I don't know if you can manage to find somewhere to sit—"

He threw a bundle of science magazines on the floor, leaving a space on the corner of his desk. He cleared a low filing cabinet for Clinton, sat himself on the desk, and motioned Slade to the chair.

"Is it necessary to dig up the past?" he asked, coming to the point.

"I'm afraid so. You must understand I have no wish to be unpleasant about this investigation, Setchley. But murder is murder."

The chemist frowned gloomily at the magazines he had dislodged.

"I appreciate that. But you see, Inspector, all of us who knew Kindilett in the old days—well, we have a secret understanding to save his feelings. You understand? Mary was the apple of his eye. She was a nice girl, jolly, gay, a bit independent, but every one liked her?"

"She was popular?"

"Immensely. I think the whole team was in love with her. When they found her after that dance it hit us all pretty hard. But Kindilett—it broke his life till he began afresh, building the Trojans. That's why he found so much loyalty among those who knew him in the old days. He'd had a bad break, and some of us felt we should rally round. I don't want to get sentimental, but we feel some loyalty to him. Sympathy too, if you like."

There was just a shade of defiance in Setchley's manner, as though he expected to be misunderstood. He was a scientist, a man without a great deal of sentiment in his nature, and he was rather shy in making this admission.

"You, Morring, and Doyce," said Slade.

"Not Doyce. He came along afterwards. I don't think Kindilett was too keen to have him, although he realized his quality as a player. But he offered no objection. It was Morring who objected, very firmly. I was the one who was directly responsible for Doyce being in the Trojans. He was a good player. To me that was what counted. I couldn't see that his private life was anyone's concern save his own. It certainly wasn't mine."

"Then you mean you and Morring rallied round Kindilett when he proposed forming the Trojans."

"Yes. But don't forget Raille. Without Raille there would have been no team. He was with Kindilett at the beginning of the Trojan venture."

"But Raille wasn't a member of the Saxon Rovers in Kindilett's time?"

"No. But he was in the Saxon Amateurs. They were a sort of off-shoot of the other team, affiliated as a kind of nursery club. That's where Raille got his grounding in soccer, and imbibed Kindilett's own principles."

"Would Raille have known Mary Kindilett?"

"I don't think there can be any doubt. Every man in both teams knew her. But you won't find Raille any more ready to talk than the rest of us. He's very loyal to Kindilett, shares his ideals about the Trojans. In fact, he makes the team, as a working unit, possible. He's with Kindilett when there's any foreign soccer manager over here, explaining things, boosting the team's stock. Raille's a hard worker. He was going the rounds with Kindilett only last week. The manager of some Swedish team, from Stockholm I believe, was interested in the Trojans. They all came along here, saw me. They called on other members of the team. Plenty of hard work keeping that sort of thing going, holding a team together, and then having to make sure it's up to scratch, fit and ready for a tussle like Saturday."

Setchley spoke with warmth. It was plain that he was a soccer enthusiast, and it was not difficult to see that a man of his type would try hard to win a place in the team for a good player such as Doyce. Setchley was single-minded, like most scientists. He concerned himself with facts more than theories. He was materialist rather than dreamer and idealist.

"That certainly enables me to get a better idea of your team as a working unit, to use your own phrase," Slade told him.

He nodded.

"Now, to get to the real reason for your visit, Inspector," he said, his manner becoming matter-of-fact. "The aconitine we had here in the lab. is missing. I don't know when it went. Tompkins doesn't know. We've tried to think when either of us saw it last—consciously, to remember it, I mean. Six weeks is the nearest we can say with surety. I know that's hopeless for your investigation, but then I don't want to think that was the stuff that—"

He spread his hands in a gesture of distaste.

"May I see the poison cabinet?" Slade asked.

"Certainly. Come right through. Tompkins is in the lab. now, working on something."

He led them into an apartment gleaming with glass and metal. On a zinc-covered bench a bunsen hissed, and a spectacled young man was holding a test-tube of coloured liquid in the flame. He didn't look round when the three men entered. Only when Setchley addressed him did he turn his head.

"These are officers from Scotland Yard, Tompkins. They're here to find out what happened to that aconitine."

The young man blinked through the thick lenses of his glasses, and smiled a toothy smile.

"They're out of luck," he stated flatly. "I don't know. It's not in the cabinet over there, and it's not anywhere else in the lab. Their guess is as good as mine."

Setchley showed the Yard men the poison cabinet. It was fixed to the wall over a small desk. He opened it. Rows of bottles and jars with neat labels stood on narrow shelves.

"That's where the aconitine was."

He pointed to a gap on a shelf.

"How long ago was it you were on that experiment with the stuff?" asked Slade.

"Oh, all of six months. But Tompkins remembers it was here six weeks ago."

The assistant put down the test-tube in a rack, turned low the bunsen's flame, and wandered over towards the group in front of the cabinet.

"That's right," he affirmed. "I checked all the stuff six weeks ago. It was there then."

"And you've no idea when it was taken?"

"If it was taken—no," said Tompkins.

"How do you mean," said Slade sharply, "if it was taken?"

"Well, a cleaner might have had an accident and kept quiet about it."

"Not likely the accident would be just to that bottle," said Slade. "Others on the shelf would have been broken too."

Tompkins nodded. "I guess so," he agreed. He frankly had little interest in the Yard men's investigation. Clinton glared at him as though his attitude were an affront.

"Didn't break it yourself, by any chance?" snapped the sergeant.

Tompkins turned on his supercilious smile.

"Not that I'm aware of," he said, and sauntered back to the bunsen.

Slade grinned. It was seldom Clinton got no change out of people he questioned. He turned to Setchley, grave again.

"It was last Monday when Morring called about the insurance, wasn't it?"

Setchley's eyes narrowed.

"Yes."

"Did he come in here?"

The chemist hesitated, reluctant to give a reply.

"As a matter of fact, he did. It was against this desk that I tripped and bruised my chest."

"Was he alone in here at any time?"

"Look here, Inspector, I protest against—"

"Against what?"

Setchley shrugged helplessly. "Oh, what's the good?" he said resignedly. "But you're barking up the wrong tree. He was alone in here for a minute or two, but I tell you—"

He shrugged again. A look at Clinton had discovered vast satisfaction on the sergeant's square face.

"And Kindilett, when he came with Raille and the Swedish manager. He in here too?"

"Yes. But not alone. I was talking to the Swede most of the time."

"And your attention wouldn't have been on the cabinet?"

"No, naturally not."

"Your assistant?"

"You'd better ask him," Setchley suggested.

But Tompkins, when he dragged his attention away from the test-tube he was heating, had noticed nothing. Slade did not find it difficult to believe him.

They went back to Setchley's cubby-hole of an office.

"What do you make of it?" the chemist asked. "You've certainly got some prime suspects now—me, Morring, Kindilett, Raille. Better include the whole team, and take your pick."

His laugh was edged.

Slade surprised him by switching to a completely different subject.

"Who was Mary Kindilett's fiancé?"

Setchley looked at the speaker suspiciously.

"I don't know. Did you expect me to?"

"I thought you might know, that's all."

"Any special reason?" He seemed determined to press the point.

"None, except no one else seems to know the man's identity. I thought you might possibly be an exception."

"Sorry to disappoint you. I'm not. Don't think I'm touchy, but there's a bit of mystery about that subject. I don't think even her father knows to whom she was engaged."

"You said she was independent. That certainly sounds like it," the sergeant agreed.

"Morring and Raille?" queried Slade.

"You can ask them. I don't think they know. Don't see why they should if the rest of us didn't learn it at the time of the inquest."

"Doyce? Would he have known?"

Setchley drew himself together.

"Look here," he said, "I can't honestly help you with these questions. If I could I would. I don't know who knows. I don't, and that's all I care about."

They left shortly after that. Clinton was openly sarcastic.

"That's what is called aiding the police," he grunted. "We could have got more help out of a sick headache. As for that assistant, Tompkins, with his buck teeth and goggle eyes. I'd like to—"

He breathed hard.

"But it's another chalk against Morring," he added.

"That should please you," said Slade, starting the car.

They had a meal in a small restaurant off the Haymarket, and went back to the Yard. Purposely they kept off the subject of their investigation, even when Slade bought an evening paper and the headline "Yard Men in Provinces: New Turn to Arsenal Mystery" shrieked at them from the front page. For nearly an hour Slade was with the Assistant-Commissioner. The A.C. was inclined superficially to find fault and pick holes.

"We've got to avoid chasing our tails in this case, Slade," he said. "There mustn't be any running round in circles."

Slade knew the A.C. well. This seeming querulousness hid a nervous tension that had to be relieved. The man lived with a dozen cases each day. He was entitled to his grumble.

"I've looked at your reports. Seems plain to me, we've got a case against Philip Morring. What do you think?"

Here was the difficulty Slade had foreseen in having to report at this stage in the case.

"I think we ought to take a little longer," he said bluntly. "The case against Morring is circumstantial—strong, but still circumstantial. I'd like to find the weapon before we make a decided step."

The A.C. frowned.

"You realize of course that by this time the murderer has probably thrown whatever poisoned object pricked Doyce into the Thames."

"That's a possibility. But somehow I don't think so," said Slade slowly.

"Reason?"

"I don't think the murderer would have risked concealing the sharp object on his person, for one thing. Suppose they had all been searched. He wasn't to know. It would have been conclusive proof. On the other hand, with it concealed in a pocket, suppose some one jogged against him, or he stumbled, in the dressing-room, while changing, or on the field of play—that would be suicide, no less."

The A.C. nodded.

"There's something in that," he agreed. "But what is your own idea, Slade?"

He knew Slade's methods and the way the detective's mind worked. Numerous cases in the past, now successfully closed in Scotland Yard's records, attested to the efficiency of the chief of Department X2. Occasionally Slade's methods had not been those of the copybook. Sometimes he had run an apparent risk, but invariably he had been able to justify what he had done, and, more important, produce a result that would stand up in court.

As the A.C. knew full well, the Yard's field workers had not only to complete a case, but they had to complete a case in such a way that it remained legally sound. A case, however brilliant the deduction and detective work involved, was of no practical use if its method of solution allowed a defence counsel to get up and shoot it full of legal holes.

In the past Slade's cases had been presented in court with such finality of evidence that there had been no doubts in the open minds of the jury. The A.C., out of past experience of his man and his achievements, was content to let Slade work things out in his own way. As a police official, he was satisfied that Slade would produce a sound and airtight case when he had marshalled his facts; as a student of psychology, he was interested in the human values on which Slade concentrated.

He considered the detective's reply very closely.

"I believe," said Slade, "that the weapon—to continue to use that term—is still at the Arsenal Stadium. The murderer, I am positive, retrieved it and concealed it somewhere, waiting an opportunity to get it away unperceived—"

"Surely he would have done that to-day," the A.C. objected.

"I don't think so."

"Then you think you know where it is?"

"I do."

The A.C. had followed the reports closely. "You've only one room sealed—the treatment room," he reflected. "So you think it's there?"

"Yes. It would have been too risky hiding it in either of the dressing-rooms. There were too many men about. It was asking for failure." He paused, added thoughtfully, "But I shall cover the visitors' dressing-room again—in case."

"But he could have taken it out on the ground and pressed it into the turf. It couldn't have been a big object. It had to fit that envelope."

"Even that was risky," Slade pointed out. "There were seventy thousand people watching the game. Any attempt to get rid of the object in that fashion would have been noticed. I admit the player—if the murderer is a player—could have stooped to tie his boot, and surreptitiously pushed the object, obviously sharp, into the ground. But would he risk even that? The game is speedy. In a matter of seconds the ball might swing his way, and he might find himself in the centre of some strenuous play with the object in his hand. A prick, and—"

Slade left the rest unspoken. The A.C. frowned.

"You think you've got the murderer summed up pretty well, eh?"

"I think I know the way his mind would tick—after the crime. If the object were hidden in the turf it would have to be during the second half. And Doyce had not fallen when the players trooped on to the field. Suppose, by some outside chance, he hadn't pricked himself? Could the murderer risk losing the object altogether without *knowing*?"

The A.C. acknowledged this point with a short nod.

"That's reducing the murderer's perspective very narrowly," he said. "Risky from our point of view. And he apparently had a fair supply of the poison."

"I don't think he would have gone through all this dramatic preparation a second time," Slade said. "The whole affair has an element of climax about it. I am sure that whatever the murderer's object was, it meant something to Doyce. It was something that would hold a strange personal significance for him."

"How do you make that out?"

"The Press cutting suggests as much."

The A.C. considered this.

"Isn't that rather clouding the issue?" he asked.

"Frankly, I don't think so. Rather the reverse. That cutting has a definite value in the case. Its value is related to some other value—I am presuming the value of the weapon employed—"

"I don't follow you there, Slade."

The detective smiled. "I was hoping to keep this back until I had progressed a little farther," he admitted, "but I can see I had better show my hand."

The A.C. looked interested. "You've got something, then?"

"I've got this much," said Slade. "Mary Kindilett was engaged in rather mysterious circumstances. Her father, I am informed, didn't know the name of her fiancé. The engagement was broken off. Doyce took her to a dance, and she did not return home. She was found drowned. At the inquest the fiancé did not come forward. Doyce is murdered four years later and a cutting refer-ring to the tragedy sent him with an object that killed him. That object is related to the cutting in some way. At least, I am assum-ing as much."

"Yes, I follow all that," said the A.C. slowly. "And your assump-tion is reasonable. I see that now. But you haven't told me any-thing new."

"My point is this," Slade resumed. "I believe the object that killed Doyce was no less than Mary Kindilett's engagement ring."

The A.C. started.

"Good God, man, but—why?"

"It's the only 'weapon' that fits in with the dramatic back-ground of the crime—Doyce's first match in Kindilett's team, the Press cutting, his death on the field of play, and one other important thing."

"Well?"

Little creases showed at the corners of the A.C.'s eyes. He was following Slade's argument with closest attention, and he saw that there was a good deal to what the detective claimed. At first it sounded fantastic, unsubstantiated, something with little more foundation than a hunch, but now he could see where Slade's emphasis on human values was evolving a reasoned explanation.

"How was the murderer to be certain that Doyce would not show the object to his team-mates? He couldn't be sure unless the object was something—considered in conjunction with the cut-ting—about which Doyce would wish to remain silent. Anyway, until he had tried to work out the reason for the package, the ring, and the cutting."

"Yes, that's a strong point," the A.C. conceded. "Doyce would have put such a ring in his pocket. It wasn't found there."

"Because the murderer had taken it. That again points to the treatment room. Doyce's clothes were hung up there."

"The room was locked, remember."

"Afterwards. There was an interval. There must have been. Allison did not 'phone immediately. Then there was another interval during which the clothes were removed from the dressing-room to the treatment room. Anyone could have had an opportunity to take the ring from a pocket—except the Arsenal players themselves. They were in their own dressing-room all the time after the match. As you know, the evidence of Punch McEwan and the commissionaire shows that no one got to the dressing-rooms between half-time and the end of the game, unless he left the field of play and entered by the players' corridor. But Doyce himself was the only one who left the field."

The A.C. stroked his jaw.

"It's a devil of a problem, put like that, Slade," he confessed. "But"—his tone sharpened—"you said just now 'if the murderer is a player.' What did you mean exactly?"

Slade considered his next words carefully.

"There's a strong presumptive case against Kindilett himself," he said slowly, "in view of what we turned up at Ryechester."

The A.C. considered this for some moments.

"Yes—I see." He took a turn across the office. "And you propose?"

"Seeing Kindilett to-night. Putting the cutting, newspaper report of the inquest, and photo in front of him, and getting his reaction. If he isn't our man, he may be suspecting something. He may be holding something back."

"Why should he?"

"I shouldn't be surprised if he mistrusted Doyce. That fatal dance must have rankled with him. It looks as though Doyce may have been instrumental in breaking up the mysterious engagement and disturbing the girl's mind. She went with him to the dance. That suggests the pendulum swinging over in—well, mental reaction."

"And Morring?" snapped the A.C., getting back to the original case he had considered.

"He remains where he was."

"And supposing he was Mary Kindilett's fiancé?"

"Then we'll have to arrest him," Slade concluded, not attacking this supposition as he had when Clinton raised it.

The A.C. sighed and sat down. He spent a short while looking at his fingers.

"All right," he said at last, "carry on along those lines, Slade, but be careful—though I don't need to give you that caution. Don't give too much away."

"I shan't do that," Slade assured him. "I was tempted at first to show the cutting to Allison, in case it meant anything to him. But he's Kindilett's friend. It would have been placing him in an unnecessarily awkward position."

"Good. Keep your lines clear, whatever you do. And now is there anything else?"

"Yes. I've got a suggestion."

"What is it?"

"I believe the murderer took the aconitine from Setchley's lab. When I find that person I'll have the murderer. But I've got to make him show himself. One way of doing that is to give that sealed treatment room publicity. The inquest is to-morrow morning. I think we could have the coroner make an announcement about an impending arrest, and then bring in an adjournment, in the public interest."

"Why say anything about an arrest?"

"I want to give the murderer food for thought. I want him to think he's slipped up somewhere. We can put the information in such a way that he will work out his danger for himself."

"You think that'll send him to the treatment room in double quick time?"

"I'll go over it first—every inch. Also the visitors' dressing-room."

"You've been over them once."

"Yes, on Saturday. But this will be a longer job."

"I see. And the murderer gets his chance to put the noose round his neck when?"

"Wednesday morning. He'll be well worked up by then, with Press statements and another day to get restive in."

"And suppose he's not such a fool, Slade?"

"I don't think he's a fool. But equally I don't think he'll let another man take the blame for himself. Whoever he is, I think he considers himself morally justified in what he's done. Probably considers himself an arbiter of justice."

"What are you driving at? Come to the point. I won't bite."

Slade smiled. "If in the course of the next thirty-six hours Morring is subjected to special attention that will be all that's wanted to make sure."

The A.C. stared.

"Morring! But he's—" He broke off, regarded Slade severely. "Then you're convinced Morring isn't guilty?"

"If he was engaged to Mary Kindilett, as I said, we'll have to arrest him. The case against him can't be broken, *if* he was the girl's fiancé. If he wasn't, then I'm certain he isn't guilty. I can't bring myself to believe in so much coincidence as stands out in the case against him."

Again the A.C. got to his feet.

"This is asking rather much, Slade."

"It is an unusual case," the detective pointed out. "We haven't a husband who's killed his wife and buried her in the garden. This murder was done openly. No attempt to make it look like accident. No cover-up. Just murder, with the murderer showing his crime and concealing himself. That reveals a state of mind. It's the state of mind I'm trying to alter. Then I'll be able to get my real proof."

"If it doesn't come off we've lost valuable time. It's a gamble."

"That's the very reason why our man will be inveigled into doing something. This whole affair has been a moral gamble on his part."

For a couple of minutes the A.C. tramped the carpet. Finally he came to a pause opposite the detective.

"Very well, I'll get the Commissioner on the 'phone and fix things. For all our sakes, Slade, I hope you're right."

Slade went thoughtfully back to his own office. Clinton had gone. He 'phoned Kindilett's hotel.

"I'd like to see you for a few minutes, Mr Kindilett," he explained. "I've one or two things to show you."

"Show me?"

The Trojan manager sounded interested.

"Yes. I want your advice."

"Then you've been digging up things in Ryechester? I saw the notice in the evening paper."

The football manager's tone was faintly accusatory.

"I quite understand how you must feel about this, Mr Kindilett," said the Yard man diplomatically, "but I have a direct lead that makes this interview to-night rather imperative."

"Can't it wait until after the inquest? I'm very tired."

"It could," Slade replied cautiously, realizing that the other man's manner was now somewhat hostile, "but your help now might obviate unpleasant publicity to-morrow."

That left Kindilett in two minds. There was a pause, then he said, "Very well, I'll wait up. When are you coming?"

"Immediately," said Slade and hung up.

XII

A Conspiracy of Circumstances

FRANCIS KINDILETT WAS STAYING IN A SMALL BLOOMSBURY hotel that catered well for its guests and gave them, in addition, the seclusion of an ancient tree-lined thoroughfare. Slade found the Trojan manager in a room near the top of the building, from the window of which he could watch the crimson gleam of distant neon lighting.

"You certainly lost no time," said Kindilett when the Yard man appeared.

He seemed, to Slade, to have recovered somewhat from his hostile reception on the telephone. The Yard man noticed fresh lines in the other's face, and shrewdly guessed that what he had read in the evening papers had been a shock to the man.

"I'm afraid my mission isn't altogether a pleasant one, Mr Kindilett. I must ask you to tell me the circumstances surrounding your daughter's death four years ago."

Kindilett took it well.

"This course is necessary, Inspector?" he asked, his voice betraying no emotion.

"I'm sorry, yes," Slade said.

They sat down. Slade took a cigarette from Kindilett's proffered case.

"Very well." Kindilett blew out the match he had struck. "How do I start?"

"First, you recognize this photograph, I suppose."

Slade produced the photograph the editor of the *Ryechester Chronicle* had given him. Kindilett looked at it, nodded.

"I recognize the players—at least, some of them. I can't say I remember the photograph. There were quite a number taken in the old days, of course. Also, quite a few players came into the team and left, with each season."

"Naturally. That is your daughter?"

"Yes." Kindilett's face was a mask. "That is Mary. And that is Hodgson and Barnes. And there is Setchley. He's changed a bit. Those are Saxon Rovers, as you probably are aware, Inspector."

"The man at the opposite end from your daughter. Do you recognize him, Mr Kindilett?"

"No, I can't say I do. But then I don't recall that player second from the left in the front row. And that man with the bushy hair at the back escapes me."

Slade took the photograph, put it on one side. He offered Kindilett the Press cutting found in Doyce's pocket.

"I found this in John Doyce's clothes when I searched them on Saturday."

Kindilett started as he read the few words.

"But I don't understand. You mean—"

"Here is a report on the inquest. I need not say any more, I know. You will see that this cutting is taken from that report—from a copy some one had presumably kept."

The Trojan manager's hands trembled.

"This is incredible!" he murmured. "I can't believe it, Inspector."

"Nevertheless, it is true. In the package that came for Doyce was this cutting. It was obviously intended to refresh his memory. Whoever killed him, Mr Kindilett, was well aware of what happened in Ryechester four years ago, and presumably wished to remind Doyce just before he died."

There was silence for some moments while Kindilett's eyes travelled the columns of print.

"Well," he said, "what do you wish me to say? I—I can assure you I don't know what to say. This is beyond me. I can't fathom it at all."

"Did you know to whom your daughter was engaged?"

Kindilett looked up.

"No," he said, very quietly, but his voice was not quite even.

"Mr Kindilett," said Slade gravely, "I must ask you to tell me the truth concerning your daughter's death. After careful consideration of the facts, as I know them, I believe that the circumstances of her death have a definite bearing on the murder of John Doyce."

The room was warm, but Kindilett shivered as he lifted his gaze.

"You really believe that?"

"I do," the Yard man said. "I'll be more explicit. I believe Doyce was murdered by means of a ring that was sent to him. A ring with one of its claws prised up, and that claw smeared with poison. It pricked Doyce's thumb as he opened the envelope containing it. He died within an hour of pricking his thumb. With the ring was the Press cutting alluding to your daughter's death. Now you'll understand why I must learn the truth about your daughter. It may be the vital link in a chain of evidence that will convict Doyce's murderer."

Kindilett ran a hand over his grey head. While Slade had been talking he had slumped farther down in his chair. It seemed as though he had not heard the detective's words. Slade, knowing how hard he was taking this, gave him time. Finally, as Slade did not continue, Kindilett roused himself and spoke.

"I understand—now," he said. There was a great weariness in his voice, a weariness not of the body only. He appeared to brace himself before continuing. "Mary was a vivacious girl, 'modern' in the best sense of the word. She was independent by nature, and like a lot of girls in these days thought she was at the same time emotionally independent of every one and everything. She had her feet on the ground, however, and her brain was clear-thinking." He paused. "Another cigarette, Inspector?"

"No, thank you."

"A drink, perhaps?"

"Not just now, thanks."

Kindilett nodded, and without further preamble resumed. "Naturally, as I was a member of the Saxon Rovers' board, Mary attended many of the games with me. She knew all about the team, liked talking to the players, and was keen on soccer. The players liked her. I know that some of them rather admired her. She was a good-looking girl, with poise and a smile that for me was always charming. I was proud of her, Inspector."

The simple statement rang with sincerity. But Slade, watching the man's pale face, saw fresh lines of strain. He knew that Kindilett was opening spiritual wounds.

When he resumed the Trojan manager seemed oblivious of the detective's presence. He neither looked at Slade nor appeared to be addressing him. Slade had the uncanny feeling that the man was soliloquizing. He spoke his feelings rather than his thoughts.

"One day," he went on, "Mary came to me and told me she was in love. I shall never forget the look in her eyes at that moment or the light in her face. I didn't question the truth of what she told me. I could see it. I told her I was glad, and asked her who was the lucky man. And that was where my girl ran true to form, Inspector. She would have her little joke. She wouldn't tell me. I had to find out for myself, she said. Well, a few days later she had a solitaire engagement ring on her finger. She was more proud of it than she would have been of the Koh-i-noor. But still she wouldn't tell me the name of her fiancé."

As he paused Slade said, "You guessed?"

Kindilett shook his head.

"Frankly, Inspector, I couldn't. I had a feeling that he might be a footballer—"

"One of the Saxon Rovers?"

The grey head nodded.

"Yes," Kindilett admitted.

"Doyce?" probed Slade.

Kindilett's shoulders squared. For a moment he looked angry, but when he spoke his voice was controlled.

"I don't know," he said.

"Morring?"

Kindilett took a deep breath, his lips twitched.

"It's no use," he said. "I don't know and I can't tell you, Inspector. It might have been anyone in the team. But that is only my—my feeling. It might have been no one in the team. She never told me. I have never known. Two days after I first saw the ring on her finger it was gone. That light, too, had gone from her eyes. But she would not tell me of her trouble. Her pride refused to let her. That, again, was Mary running true to form. I remember once when she was a child of six or seven, and some one accidentally broke a favourite doll—But no matter," he broke off, gesturing with a hand. "I could see she had been hurt deeply. But I knew that she was determined not to let anyone know, not even me. That made me very sad, Inspector. I knew then that she would never tell me the name of the man."

Kindilett rose, walked to the window, and for some moments stared at the red haze in the distant sky. When he resumed his back remained towards the detective.

"She went to a dance one night with John Doyce. She did not come back. You know what happened."

The voice was the voice of a broken man.

"Who do you think killed Doyce?" asked Slade, speaking very quietly.

The man at the window trembled.

"I don't know."

The words were complete negation. Slade studied the man's back, the droop of the square shoulders.

"You never liked Doyce, did you?" he asked.

"I am not aware that I ever evinced any animosity towards him."

"That doesn't alter the fact that you never liked him, as, say, you liked Morring?"

Kindilett half turned.

"Why keep alluding to Morring?"

"Do I?"

"I—Perhaps I was mistaken. I appreciated Doyce's qualities as a footballer, but—"

"You know something of his reputation with women?"

"Inspector, must we continue in this strain? I find it decidedly unpleasant."

Kindilett was himself again. He came back to his chair, manner cool, eyes alert, watchful, the creases still deep round his eyes and at the sides of his mouth.

"I'm sorry," Slade apologized, a little too easily. "But as controller of the team I took it that you could help me place the individuals in it—"

"Inspector," said Kindilett, "what are you trying to get me to say? Out with it, please."

Slade considered his man.

"Mind if I light my pipe?" he asked.

"Not at all. Go ahead."

Slade lit his pipe, cradled the bowl in the fingers of his left hand. By the time he spoke he had carefully trimmed what he was about to say.

"You could tell me if anyone in the team had a grudge against Doyce."

"You asked that same question of Raille this morning, if I am not mistaken."

"I did. And I got the impression that Raille was withholding facts he could have told me. I realized his position, employed by the club. He could believe that a somewhat binding loyalty was expected of him."

"Yet not of me?"

There was a faintly ironic smile on Kindilett's face.

"I must get the truth somewhere, Mr Kindilett. You are the man to tell me. I believe Doyce was hated by some one in the team, some one who knew your daughter well—"

Slade hesitated. Kindilett, in the same ironic mood, was quick to point out what Slade had left unsaid.

"That could very well suggest me," he said.

"You did not kill Doyce?"

It was a plain question, simply asked.

"Would you believe me," countered Kindilett, "if I said no and circumstances conspired to make it seem that I lied?"

Slade acknowledged this riposte with a tight smile.

"That is a shrewd thrust. One it is not quite fair to expect me to answer."

"I see." Kindilett was openly mocking now. "Very well, I'll give you a categorical answer to your own question, Inspector—no."

Slade rose. "I'm afraid I've kept you rather longer than I had anticipated, Mr Kindilett. I'm sorry—"

"Please don't apologize, Inspector. I understand your position, and it is one I do not envy you. Now, a drink before you leave?"

Slade looked into the pale eyes with the hint of mockery still in their depths and revised his decision.

"Thank you," he said.

Kindilett produced whisky and glasses. They drank solemnly, and Slade took his departure, feeling that perhaps he had not had altogether the best of the encounter.

He called back at the Yard, to leave the photograph and Press extracts, and found a surprise awaiting him in the persons of Philip Morring and Jill Howard. He glanced at his watch.

"I know it's awfully late, Inspector," said the girl, "but this is important."

The detective glanced at Morring. The footballer's dinner jacket fitted him perfectly, and he made a handsome companion for the girl, who was plainly responsible for the visit. It did not take a detective to deduce that they had been out somewhere and had been discussing the general situation, and the girl had persuaded Morring to call at the Yard without delay.

"Very well, let's hear what it's all about."

They sat down in Slade's office, and the tired detective tried afresh to bring an unblunted intelligence to the understanding of this new situation. This was the second time, he reflected, that Morring had voluntarily come forward.

"First of all," said the girl, "I'm responsible for this late visit."

The admission brought a smile to Slade's face.

"I had suspected that, Miss Howard."

The girl blushed, but went on, undaunted.

"Miss Laruce threatened to come to you and try to make things look black for Mr Morring—"

"Jill, I say," Morring protested, shamefaced at this outright championing.

"Why should she do that?" asked Slade, keeping a straight face.

"Because—" The girl stopped, suddenly embarrassed under the detective's frank scrutiny. "Phil, you'll have to tell him—but tell him everything," she added hurriedly.

Unhappily Morring took up his tale.

"I'm afraid Miss Laruce was not quite candid with you, Inspector—"

"When do you mean?" Slade inquired blandly, now enjoying himself. "Yesterday or when she called upon me to-day?"

Blank looks masked the faces of his two visitors.

"I told you—" began the girl, only to stop again.

But Slade's intimation produced a subtle change in Morring. The footballer accepted the implication and took up its challenge.

"I see. She has corrected a few wrong impressions she gave you on Sunday."

"Such was her intention, as she gave me to understand," said Slade.

"In that case," Morring continued, "I can get straight to the point. I did quarrel with Doyce about my fiancée. I considered his conduct objectionable, and told him so—er—in no uncertain terms is the customary cliché, I believe."

"I take it you told him to be careful or next time he'd have more painful reason to regret his—um—interference?"

The two men grinned, while the girl looked from one to the other, wide-eyed, unable to appreciate a humour that was essentially masculine.

"I told him I'd knock his face in—or worse."

"What I meant," nodded Slade. "And one can't insure smashed faces."

"Film stars can," Morring pointed out.

Slade nodded again. "I was forgetting them. It must be the late hour. Is there anything else to tell me?"

"Only that I would have kept my word had I known about Friday and—and the rest of it. But I didn't know. On Sunday I broke off my engagement to Miss Laruce. We were engaged, despite any 'impression' you received at the flat. And now—er—I don't think I'll keep you any longer from your bed, Inspector. You must have had a long day, with the trip to Ryechester, and—"

"But, Phil," the girl protested, "you haven't told the Inspector about calling at Mr Setchley's laboratory, and—"

She stopped. There was a grim look on Morring's face.

"I think he knows all about that, Jill," he said quietly. "Anyway, we're a bit late with that sort of explanation."

Slade looked from one to the other. He saw that this dark-haired girl was alive to any danger threatening the man, and keen to warn him, protect him if she could. It was not difficult for Slade to read into this the truth of the girl's affection for Morring.

"There is something you can help me about, I think," said the detective, abruptly changing the subject. "I've been trying to get a line on Mary Kindilett's fiancé. Can you help me, Morring?"

Morring's head shook.

"No. I don't know who he was."

"That's what every one says."

Morring's mouth twisted at one side.

"They could be telling the truth," he suggested.

It was a point to him. Slade acknowledged this with a grin.

"That's the devil of it," he admitted. Then with great casualness, "But wait a minute. There's something else. You might still be able to help me. Take a look at this."

He showed Morring the photograph.

"That's Mary Kindilett?"

"Yes."

"And the man at the end? The one in ordinary clothes. Recognize him?"

There was a pause.

"No," said Morring, when his mind seemed made up.

"You can't place him?" Slade pressed.

"No. I won't say I haven't seen him before. But four years ago, and I might have seen him only once—you know how it is."

Slade nodded heavily.

"Yes, I know how it is," he echoed, and his tone brought a flush to the footballer's face.

"What does this picture mean?" asked the girl, determined not to be left out of anything that affected Morring in the eyes of the police.

"I don't know, Jill—"

"I'll tell you, Miss Howard," said Slade, turning to the girl.

"Four years ago Mary Kindilett was found drowned. She had been engaged and she broke off the engagement suddenly, without explanation. The night before her body was discovered she went to a dance with John Doyce."

While he was speaking Slade watched Morring's face. The footballer was frowning, but he did not reveal any deep emotion, as Slade had half hoped.

"How terrible!" said the girl. "Then you think Mary Kindilett's fiancé—whoever he is—"

"He may have been dead for years," said Morring flatly, interrupting her.

"I don't think so," said Slade.

That ended the interview. He got no more out of them, and they found him unprepared to talk about the morrow's inquest.

Shortly after they had gone Slade sought the comfort of his own bed. He did not sleep well.

XIII

Bait

THE WELL OF THE COURT WAS CROWDED FOR THE INQUEST on John Doyce. The Press seats were full, and Slade, glancing round at the sea of faces, made out the Trojan and Arsenal teams, Patricia Laruce, some distance away Jill Howard, and in one corner of the court the spectacled face of the editor of the *Ryechester Chronicle*, Whittaker and Raille he saw there together, chatting in low tones. There was a good number of women present.

He turned an eye to the jury, sitting there with contented looks on their faces. The foreman was constantly throwing a quick glance at George Allison, where the Arsenal manager sat with Francis Kindilett. Slade could well understand what was in the man's mind. Here was a fine opportunity to probe into the affairs of the Arsenal Club, under the guise of asking pertinent questions.

There were quite a few people in that court, Slade felt, who were going to be disappointed, including the foreman of the jury. The coroner, a bald-headed ex-Army surgeon who knew how to handle recalcitrant jurymen, came in and took his seat, and proceedings started. The formalities were quickly run through. The jury filed out and viewed the body. Francis Kindilett officially identified the corpse, and Dr Meadows came forward and gave his evidence.

Morring was called, and said a brief piece. The foreman of the jury was ready to prolong Morring's ordeal, but the coroner dealt drastically with him. Morring left his seat.

As he did so Clinton, timing his interruption with clockwork precision, pushed forward and placed a piece of paper in front of the coroner, who put on his glasses and read it carefully through, as though he had not already been told on the 'phone what it was about and what was expected of him.

The court fidgeted. The foreman of the jury—a butcher in ordinary life—resentful of the treatment meted out by the coroner, gave vocal effect to his resentment by a series of rasping coughs which resounded throughout the court.

The coroner went on reading.

Finally he looked up and said, "Ah!"

Every one sat forward, expecting a dramatic development.

"I have just had notice from the police," said the coroner. "I understand that they have very recently come by an important piece of evidence which will enable them to secure—" He hesitated, waved a hand. "Perhaps I shouldn't go into all that. The point is this."

He paused, and the fidgeting recommenced.

"The point is," he went on, "that I have a special request from the police for this inquest to be adjourned in the public interest."

The foreman was on his feet, his fleshy face mottled with indignation.

"But—but—" he got out, with seeming difficulty.

"This court will most certainly accede to this official request. The inquest on John Doyce is adjourned for a fortnight."

The coroner's gavel came down. Chairs creaked, people got up. A hubbub of talk broke out. Slade, catching Clinton's eye, motioned towards the exit. The two Yard men met.

"Nicely timed," Slade approved. "Get Raille. The papers will be sure to seize on the fact that Morring was the last one allowed to speak."

Clinton nodded, drifted away. He came back with the Trojan trainer in tow.

"You wanted me, Inspector?" asked the trainer.

"Can you spare a few minutes to come along to the Yard, Raille?"

"Why, certainly. As a matter of fact, there's no training to-day at the Arsenal Stadium. It was expected that the inquest would last—"

His spread hands might have been suggesting any time up to a full week.

"Think we surprised them all?"

Slade sounded friendly.

"Yes, I think so. Finding a clue—I mean—"

"Oh, we've dug up a few things," said Slade. "That's the reason why I want you to come along to the Yard."

They spoke about trivialities until they were in Slade's office, half an hour later. Clinton got down to a pile of papers piled up on his desk. He gave no sign that his ears were working harder than his eyes. Slade produced the Ryechester photograph.

"You've seen this morning's papers, I take it, Raille?"

"Yes, a couple of them."

"Then you know about my trip down to Ryechester?"

"Yes."

"You feel very loyal towards Kindilett?"

Raille considered the question before replying.

"We've discussed this before, I think, Inspector."

"True, we have. But I've another reason for asking now. I want to get to the bottom of what happened in Ryechester four years ago. You know to what I refer?"

Raille inclined his head. His eyes were blank.

"It isn't a subject—" he began.

Slade waved an arm.

"I know. That's the tale I get from all of you who were associated with Kindilett and the Saxon Rovers. The subject is painful. So nobody will talk. That helps me a lot."

He sounded sarcastic.

"It's understandable," Raille murmured.

"That doesn't concern me. I want you, Raille, to tell me the truth of what happened. Here—look at this paper—the *Ryechester Chronicle*. There's the same trouble that I'm suffering from now, lack of personal evidence. The coroner at that inquest had something to say about it. I'm not in a position to complain. All I can do is make an appeal. And I do—to you. You're the Trojan trainer. You're in a position to help me. You want Doyce's murderer found, don't you?"

Clinton, sitting with his hands full of loose sheets of paper, first wondered if his chief was suffering from a heat wave he himself had not noticed, then arrived at the conclusion that Slade must be playing a part. The sergeant listened even more attentively. Slade, he realized, was trying to work on the other's emotions.

"You do?" persisted the detective, as Raille remained silent.

"I want the team—cleared. But—"

"That's what I meant," put in Slade quickly. "Kindilett's got you all so keen on the team spirit that none of you can think of anything else. You're every one of you just a member of a team. A digit, as it were, in a larger number. You've lost your individuality—"

"Perhaps you don't understand, Inspector, just what the Trojans signify?" said Raille mildly.

Slade looked up.

"Perhaps I don't. But are you going to help me, Raille? I want some one to be candid. I think you're the one to open up, in the interest of your club—in your own interest."

Raille smiled.

"That's a queer way of putting it," he said.

"It's what it comes down to in the end," Slade asseverated.

The trainer sat back in a chair that was not very comfortable however one sat in it.

"All right, I'll try to help you, Inspector."

Slade brightened.

"Good! That's what I wanted to hear from you. I'll be candid, we have practically solved the case—"

Raille jerked upright again.

"You have! Then why ask me—"

"Now don't get excited," Slade soothed. "Solving a case is one thing. Proving is another. I've got to go another way to work to prove what I've solved. But I don't want to bother you with routine—"

"On the contrary, Inspector, it's no bother."

"Never mind, I'm not taking advantage of your willingness to help me in the final stages, Raille," said Slade warmly.

Clinton burrowed his face deeper into the papers, to hide a grin. Slade had cleverly worked the man into the position where he wanted him, where he could use him as an easy target at which he could direct his questions. Raille seemed to realize that he had been out-manœuvred. He sat back again, a slight frown on his face.

"Now, do you know who was engaged to Kindilett's daughter?" Slade began.

"I—"

"No denials," Slade said quickly. "What you know, man. I want to get somewhere."

Raille changed his words.

"Mary Kindilett, I believe, was engaged to a footballer. I can't tell you his name."

"Well, that's an advance, anyway," Slade admitted. "Is it true, do you think, that Kindilett himself doesn't know her fiancé's name?"

"Quite likely."

"You yourself knew Mary Kindilett well?"

"I knew her of course. But I was not in the Saxon Rovers proper. I was—"

"I know. In the Saxon Amateurs, a sort of nursery club."

"You've certainly got your information complete from one angle, Inspector."

"But because you weren't in the Rovers," Slade went on, "it seems to me you might have noticed more than a man in the Rovers—say, Setchley."

Raille half smiled.

"I can't say about that, Inspector. At the time you speak of I was thinking of getting married myself. You see, I wasn't a whole-time footballer—not even as much as a player in the Rovers. I was training to be a dentist. I—well, I found it wanted money, and—er—other things, which I hadn't got."

"Thanks," said Slade. "I wasn't meaning to pry into your own private life, Raille—"

"That's all right, Inspector. It's in the past. I'm no longer sensitive. Thanks to Kindilett."

"He's been pretty good to you?"

"In various ways."

"He loved his daughter?"

"He was devoted to her."

"You think he would carry a hate with him for a long time?"

"He is a man of tireless patience, Inspector," said the trainer, picking his words with great care. "But I don't think I can answer your question. I don't know. I haven't known Francis Kindilett hate anyone."

Slade tried a fresh tack.

"Did he think Doyce morally responsible for his daughter's death? Can you tell me that?"

Raille shook his head.

"No, that's a question I am utterly unable to answer. But if you want my personal opinion—"

"Yes?"

"Then I should say no—emphatically."

"I see."

Raille glanced at Slade meaningly.

"I hope you do, Inspector. I will be frank. I think Kindilett utterly incapable of being the murderer of John Doyce."

Slade sat back.

"Well, that takes us some way along the road, Raille. I must admit that. We know where we're getting, and thanks a lot for clearing ground so rapidly. Let's take Morring, now."

Raille protested.

"You're not going through the entire team, man by man?"

"No. I don't have to."

"You don't—"

Raille sounded surprised.

"That's what I said—I don't have to. But Morring—you knew he was engaged?"

"I'd heard about it."

"You knew the girl?"

"I'd heard of her. Name of Patricia Laruce."

"You told me you called at Doyce's on Friday night, and you saw no visitor there."

"That is quite correct."

"No hat or coat lying about?"

"No. Are you suggesting I should have seen—some one?"

"I'm suggesting some one was taking good care not to be observed by you."

Raille screwed his face up in an expression of distaste.

"You don't mean—Patricia Laruce?"

"No one else. Now, Raille, do you know of anything that would point to enmity between Morring and his partner?"

Raille shook his head again.

"Nothing. I saw that they were cool to each other. I believe on Saturday Morring said something to Doyce, to which the other muttered some words I did not catch. But these are at best only impressions. I don't *know* of anything between them."

"Would it surprise you if I told you that they had already quarrelled over the girl and Morring had threatened his partner?"

"No, that wouldn't surprise me. For a long time I had an idea of the type Doyce was."

"You knew him for some time?"

"Quite a few years. But I told you this yesterday."

"I know," said Slade. "I'm just getting impressions right in my own mind. Now, please cast your mind back to your conversation with Doyce on Friday night. Was anything said that might suggest he was worried about anything—anyone?"

Raille thought back.

"Can't say I remember rightly. I went there to run the rule over him lightly. I wanted him in shape. I didn't want him tiring quickly the next day because he had spent too long up the night before. You've heard the others' opinion of him. Pretty sure of himself, over-confident. You couldn't tell him much. Had to handle him with tact."

"Just what sort of tact did you use?"

"Oh, played up to his vanity. Said the team expected his best display from him. He took it all in, even showed me his book of Press cuttings. I stayed long enough to find out there was nothing to worry about, then left."

"You were in the sitting-room of the flat?"

"Yes, the whole time."

"Did you look into his bedroom at all?"

"No, I had no reason to."

"Tell me, do you think Morring was engaged to Mary Kindilett?"

"Phil Morring?" There was more surprise in Raille's voice. "No, I—well, I—"

"I see, you hadn't considered him as a possibility?"

"No, I must confess I hadn't."

"Setchley?"

"No. But I told you, Inspector, I don't—"

"All right, I remember. Just thought you might have had an idea about one of those two. Morring especially."

"Might I inquire why?"

"Oh, just the way things are working out. It would make a good case if Morring had been engaged to her."

Slade was watching the other closely, but appearing to take an interest only in the Ryechester photograph.

"Then Morring is your number one suspect?"

"I didn't say so."

Slade looked up. He held out the photograph. "This mean anything to you?"

Raille bent over the picture.

"Mary Kindilett and some of the players."

"Know any of them?"

"Well, there's Setchley, and Barnes, I think his name was, and Hodgson, or Higginson, or some such name—"

"Don't happen to know the fellow on the right, do you? The one in civvies?"

"I can't say I do."

"Notice anything strange about Mary Kindilett?"

"Strange?"

"Yes—anything missing?"

Raille looked closer, remained looking for some moments.

"She hasn't got an engagement ring on her left hand," he said at last.

"So I noticed," said Slade. "Does that omission tell you anything?"

"No. Should it?"

"I was asking you," smiled the Yard man.

He dropped the photograph on his desk, refolded the copy of the *Ryechester Chronicle*, and rose.

"Frankly, what is your own opinion of what happened on Saturday, Raille?"

"I don't know. I've thought, but thinking hasn't got me very far, I'm afraid. I'm not cut out for a detective, any more than I was for a dentist."

For just a moment there was a lingering bitterness in his tone. Slade marked it, altered what he was about to say next.

"Who was last out of the dressing-room after half-time—remember?"

"I think I was. I was fixing a bandage round Crieff's right ankle, and we went out last. Yes, I remember now you draw my attention to it. Why?"

"None of the players lingered in the dressing-room then?"

"Not to my knowledge."

"Not Morring?"

"No, I'm sure of that."

"And Kindilett?"

"He just looked in for a moment, then went out again. I believe he had a cup of tea with Mr Allison."

"Another point, Raille. You were with Kindilett last week when he called at the laboratory in the Great West Road where Setchley works. Did Mr Kindilett appear to take an interest in the cabinet over the desk in the lab.? Did you notice?"

"Afraid I can't say. The Swedish manager of a Stockholm amateur team was there, and I remember talking about callisthenics, because the Swede was very keen on them."

"Setchley didn't happen to remark about Morring having been there the day before?"

"No. I'm sorry if I didn't notice much—"

"Oh, that's all right, Raille. Don't worry yourself. Detective work is just a case of delving and then delving again, only deeper the second time. And the third time—"

"Deeper still, eh?"

"Exactly."

Raille left shortly after that. Clinton extracted himself from his papers with a heavy sigh.

"You took him a long way round in circles," he protested vaguely.

"Bait, Clinton," said Slade. "I've sent him away to talk, to think, possibly to do some 'phoning. I've made him curious, and now—"

Clinton sucked his teeth noisily.

"Possibly a waste of time," he said unconsolingly. "Now what?"

"Now a quick visit to the Commer-Photo studio."

The Commer-Photo studio was a typical photographer's studio, untidy, littered with box-like dressing-rooms, and in the charge of a man with a very squeaky voice and an over-trimmed beard. The feminine paleness of his face above the curly beard was heightened to some extent by the brightness of his searching brown eyes.

"What has she been up to?" was his first question after the Yard men had explained the reason for their visit.

"Oh, don't get a wrong idea, Mr Sykes," said Slade. "Miss Laruce is merely required to answer a few categorical questions."

"Well, I don't like it," said the bearded Mr Sykes doggedly. "I don't have to, do I?"

"I don't like it myself," Slade confided.

Somewhat mollified by this, Mr Sykes showed the detectives into a small anteroom, with a large mirror and dressing-table, the latter littered with sundry not too clean hair-brushes, in the bristles of which were stuck coloured bath-combs. He went out and left them.

Clinton looked round the room.

"Marvellous to think anyone can make a living out of the place," he reflected.

Slade stared over the dressing-table at a particularly nauseating photograph of a stack of smoking factory chimneys. The door opened and Patricia Laruce came in. She was annoyed at their being there, and was ready to voice her grievance.

"I'll lose my job now. Sykes will go thinking I'm up to no good."

Slade forbade from telling her how right he thought she was. Instead he put on his most encouraging smile, and said, "Unfortunately I didn't get a chance to speak to you at the inquest to-day—"

"How do you know I was there?" she asked suspiciously.

"I saw you."

"Oh!"

She looked taken aback. Slade went on to seize his momentary advantage.

"I want you to cast your mind back to Friday evening."

"Friday evening?"

"Yes. John Doyce had a visitor while you were there Who was it?"

She could tell that he knew, that he was trying her out. She did not repeat her earlier mistake.

"Raille, the trainer," she said.

"He didn't see you?"

"I didn't give him the chance. I don't trust his sort."

"What sort is that?"

She shrugged and sniffed.

"I see. What did he talk about?"

"Training, being fit, playing up, playing up, and playing the game. You know the line."

"How long was he there?"

"Far too long. Nearly half an hour, I should say."

"Did you remove all your clothes into the bedroom?"

She flushed quickly. "Who said I was in the bedroom? However—" She glanced down at her smart shoes. "No, I picked up my coat, and my hat, but forgot my handbag. And now if you're finished with me—"

They were.

Outside, threading their way through the crowd that perpetually inhabits Regent Street in the daylight hours, Clinton said, "Why did Raille say he didn't know she was there?"

"Perhaps he wanted to protect her."

"Or some one else," suggested Clinton dubiously.

"Your guess is as good as mine," said Slade.

XIV

The Other Woman

UPON THEIR RETURN TO THE YARD THEY FOUND AWAITING them a communication from Milligan, the attendant at the block of flats where Doyce had lived.

The man had 'phoned about half an hour before, and would not leave a message. He wanted to speak to Inspector Slade, and had left word that what he had to say was of an urgent nature.

"Maybe something in all this Press publicity has reminded him that the rent is still overdue."

Clinton chose to take a sceptical view of the possibilities of the 'phone message.

"You know," said Slade, "I've been wondering at one aspect of this case. None of Doyce's relatives has come forward."

The sergeant perked up.

"True. But he may be an orphan."

"None of the Trojans has mentioned a word about Doyce's family."

"Well, I don't suppose this Milligan is going to confess to being a step-brother."

What Milligan had to tell them was something that made both Yard men take fresh interest in his story.

"It was just after lunch when she called," said the porter. "She was a smallish woman, pretty face, but not as young as it had been—if you know what I mean. And there was something about her eyes. I can't rightly describe them, but I remember how they looked. Hard, sort of. And fixed, too. Staring without seeming to stare, if you get me."

"I think I know what you mean, Milligan," Slade nodded.

The porter went on with his narrative.

"I saw her moving towards the lift, and not having seen her here before I thought it best to say something. You know, you can't be too careful with blocks of flats like this. All kinds of people ready to try anything. I said to her, 'Who you wanting to see, ma'am?' just like that. She fixed that hard stare on me, and said, 'Mrs Brown' quick-like, without stopping to think. She was smart, I'll say that. She had it all ready. Only it didn't do her any good. Her luck was out. There's not a Mrs Brown in the building. 'You've made a mistake,' I told her. 'We haven't got a Mrs Brown, ma'am.' She kept looking at me, and I didn't like the way she seemed to look through me. 'Maybe you've got the address wrong,' I suggested. You see, I didn't want any trouble with her, and she looked the sort to go off half-cock. You know how some women are?"

He paused, as though to make sure that Slade really did know. The Yard man nodded.

"I can see you handled her right, Milligan."

"I'm not sure I did."

"How's that?"

The man pushed his tongue into one cheek, reflected for some moments, and then took what for him was plainly a plunge into unknown depths.

"She gave me five bob and showed me a key. Wasn't any doubt about it. It was a key to Mr Doyce's flat."

"You let her go into the flat?"

"Well, I couldn't very well stop her. She said she had a perfect right, and there was the key."

"And the five bob," put in Clinton.

Milligan looked at the sergeant, and seemed to receive inspiration from the knowing look on Clinton's face.

"You see, it was like this," he said, hurrying his words. "I thought—well, if I let her in, she might do something that would give the police a clue. If I didn't let her in, chances were she'd just disappear. Then the police would know nothing. And she might be important."

He paused, uncertain how this would be taken.

"You bet she might," said Slade. "Milligan, you're a polished liar. Go on."

The porter took heart.

"Anyway, she went up. She was up there—oh, twenty minutes, not more. When she came down I came out of the office. 'Everything all right?' I inquired. Just like that. Chatty. She gave me a hell of a look. 'I've wasted five bob,' she said in a way that gave you goose-flesh. But I stuck to her. 'Taxi?' I said. 'I can get one myself,' she snapped."

"So you didn't find out where she went," Clinton gloomed.

Milligan gave a prodigious wink.

"She was fly, all right. But not fly enough. I went into the office, saw her go over to the rank, and take the first taxi. I know the driver. Bill Stevens. Him and me often has a bit of chin-wag. He's in the Auxiliary Fire Service, a part-timer, and I can't get out of him how the hell he's going to go out on a call when he's driving a fare the other side of London—"

"You know this Stevens' address?"

"No. But he works for the White Seal Cab Company. They've offices in the Euston Road."

"All right, Milligan, you've earned your five bob. But don't let anyone else up to the flat—not if they offer you a pound."

Milligan grinned. "I ain't that lucky," he told them.

The two Yard men went up to the flat, entered, and looked round the rooms.

"She has a tidy mind, whoever she is," muttered Clinton, "she's put everything back as she found it."

"Has she?" said Slade.

"Well..."

If the woman had taken anything, they couldn't tell. They left Baker Street and made their way to the Euston Road and the office of the White Seal Cab Company. A rotund Cockney in shirt-sleeves hunted up Stevens' address.

"Don't know when he'll get home. Bill's got a habit of working late. Some nights he leaves off about seven, some nights ten or later, after the theatre traffic."

"Then your drivers don't keep set hours?"

"Sure they do. But Stevens is buying a cab from the company. He's different. He works his own hours. That's why he's sticking late. Gives him a chance to pay off a bigger instalment before the cab's out of date."

The rotund man laughed. He thought that a good joke.

"Tell you what," he said, "if he happens to look in I'll get him to give you a ring. How's that?"

"It'll have to do," agreed Slade, disappointed at not finding his man sooner.

"And when we do find him he may not remember where he took her, or she may have driven to a station, just to leave a blind trail," Clinton remarked as they went in search of food.

After a meal they returned to the Yard, there to wait until word came from a taxi-driver who was cruising round London unaware that the police wanted a word with him. Slade could have got his man quicker by broadcasting the number of his cab, but he particularly wanted to keep this new lead out of the newspapers.

He was prepared to wait longer, and avoid the publicity. Already the case had enough publicity to ensure its being talked of throughout the remainder of the year.

As it happened, Slade's luck was in. An hour or so after his return to the Yard a call came through from the White Seal Cab Company, reporting that Stevens had had a breakdown, and a van had gone to tow him in. Slade and Clinton went back to the Euston Road, and found their man had just arrived, and was in a flaring temper.

"Just my confounded luck. Breakdown, an' me with rates an' taxes to pay, an' an instalment due."

The rotund man picked his teeth and winked at a mechanic.

"Take it easy, Bill. You've got all the rest of your life to wear out that cab."

"Not at the rate he's started in, he ain't," said the mechanic cheerily.

Slade and Clinton took Stevens away from the others' wit.

"Belloge Court? 'Cos I know it. Me an' Milligan the porter there are old buddies. 'Cos he's a bit of a gas-bag, an' me, I don't—"

"Remember picking up a fare while on the rank outside Belloge Court about midday?"

Stevens had no trouble in remembering. The reference to this particular fare brought a scowl to his normally bland features.

"Yes, I took her to Clifficks Gardens."

"Where's that?"

"Hampstead."

"Remember the number?"

The scowl deepened. "I shan't forget it. It brought me this bit o' bad luck. Thirteen, that was the number."

"Just one other thing," said Slade. "Did you remain outside the house in Clifficks Gardens long enough to see whether she rang the bell or used a key?"

"The whole street's blocks of flats," Stevens explained. "She just walked in through an open door. But if it means anything, she took a latch-key out of her handbag when she was standing on the kerb, about to pay me off. Put it in her mouth while she went on fumbling for change."

"Thanks," said Slade. "Er—I don't suppose you use the Belloge Court rank very often, do you?"

"As a matter of fact, I do. What with knowing Millie, an' him always bein' good for a bit o' jaw, an' there bein' a nice little cook-shop round the corner, that just suits me—well, I'm on that rank four or five times a week, I should say. Why, any particular reason?"

"I was wondering if you recalled ever picking up this same fare before. At that rank, I mean."

Stevens shook his head.

"No, can't say I can. And she was a woman one'd remember all right. Striking looking. Good eyes, bold, and she had a way with her. You know, as though she cottoned to what made the wheels go round."

"And now John Doyce. Ever had him for a fare?"

"Oh, several times. Good for a bob tip. But I don't want to get dragged into any murder case, me with that cab not paid for, and—"

"You're not being dragged into anything," Slade assured the man, who suddenly looked cagey. "I merely want to know if you ever drove Doyce to Clifficks Gardens."

Stevens shook his head.

"Never," he said, and he couldn't have put more expression into the word had he been on oath.

Slade and Clinton left the White Seal Cab Company's building.

"Hope you got what you wanted," called the shirt-sleeved man, who was still watching a mechanic work.

"Thanks for the ring," said Slade, adding nothing to satisfy the other's curiosity.

"Where does it get us?" asked Clinton, as the detectives' car sped down the Euston Road.

"To Hampstead," Slade told him, tooling his way through a crowd of traffic. Cutting north, and avoiding the West End, Slade reached Hampstead in just over a quarter of an hour. Clifficks Gardens proved to be a semicircular thoroughfare running back from the Heath.

Slade drew up before No. 13, and he and Clinton passed into a hall. On one wall was a dark brown board with the names of tenants painted in gold letters. As it happened, they were all "Mr and Mrs" save one—Mrs Edwards.

"Looks our likeliest bet," Slade agreed with Clinton, who pointed to the name.

Mrs Edwards lived in Flat 10, which proved to be at the top of a five-storey flight of stone steps. Slade rang the bell. The door opened, and they were confronted by a man in dark clothes, with a carnation in his buttonhole.

"Good afternoon, Mr Prines," said Slade. "This is a surprise."

The photographer fell back at the sight of the two Yard men.

"Good God!" he exclaimed. "What—"

"I think it would be better if we conversed inside," Slade suggested.

Reluctantly the short man allowed them entry. He was as nattily dressed as when the detectives had visited him at his studio

in Ryechester, but in place of his easy smile there was now a look
of perturbation.

"Who is it, Peter?" called a woman's voice. A deep, rich contralto.

The woman herself appeared as the Yard men entered a neatly
furnished sitting-room.

"I—"

She looked at Prines, who had followed them, after closing
the outer door. The photographer was a picture of well-dressed
dejection.

"Lily, dear, these gentlemen are police officers. I—I think they
will have some questions to ask us—er—you."

He dropped into a chair. The woman looked at her unexpected
visitors, and Slade knew what both Milligan and Stevens had meant
when they had emphasized the woman's eyes. They were large,
very blue, rather strange eyes to find in a face with such force and
strength to it. The big blue eyes of a doll-face in the face of a woman
who had personality and a will of her own.

"I am Inspector Slade of Scotland Yard," Slade introduced
himself. "This is my assistant, Sergeant Clinton. We would like
to know why you visited the flat of John Doyce and where you
procured the key."

She sat down, her back very straight.

"You are to be complimented," she said, in that same deep
contralto. "I thought I had been—circumspect." She glanced at
Prines, who now looked as though he had eaten something which
had violently disagreed with his digestion. "I was hoping to keep
out of this investigation," she told Slade, returning her attention
to the Yard man, "but I can see now that my hope was futile. I
should like to ask one question, however, before you—er—begin."

Slade inclined his head in acquiescence.

"Do you know who I am?"

She said it as though she expected to surprise her visitors.

"Well—no, to be really truthful," Slade confessed. He didn't like to say he thought she was a woman Doyce had cast off.

"I'm Mrs John Doyce."

The announcement pulled both Slade and Clinton up with a jerk. A gleam came to the sergeant's eyes.

"So he was married," he murmured.

"Do I have to produce what are popularly called one's marriage lines?" she retorted, reading into Clinton's remark something he had not meant.

"No, Mrs Doyce—"

"I prefer to be called Mrs Edwards. It's a compromise, actually. My maiden name was Edwards, but I am married."

There was a shade of defiance about the way she said this. Slade realized that he wasn't going to find this woman altogether tractable, unless she was dealt with very diplomatically.

"I think," he said, "it would be better if you told me the story in your own way, Mrs Edwards. I can see there is a story."

"A very ordinary one," she said. She sat down, smoothed her dress, and looked at them again with those strangely large eyes. She seemed to be gauging them and what she was about to say at the same time. "First let me say I come from Ryechester. That may mean something to you."

Slade acknowledged this with a nod.

"It begins to mean quite a lot," he said.

"John Doyce lost his head after Mary Kindilett's death," she went on. "I don't know why. But he did. He wasn't in love with her. He's never been in love with any woman. I know that now—or, rather, I've known it some considerable time. But I didn't know it when he began coming into the saloon bar of the Fox and Ferret. You see, I was a barmaid there."

She gave the information simply, without trying to lend the words any false meaning.

"He was fascinating, vital, and very interesting to me, who had seen nothing of life outside Ryechester, which is really a very circumscribed country town."

"Er—pardon me," Slade interrupted. "May I ask how you came to be a barmaid?"

She smiled. She was sensitive of the implied compliment in the detective's question.

"My father was a school-teacher. He died of cancer, and had not been able to save much. I just had to turn to and take the first job I could. I had no false pride."

Prines began a protest.

"Really, Lily, you don't have to—"

But she silenced him. "Peter," she said, "it isn't your husband that's been murdered, but mine. I must get my position made very clear to the police. There's plenty of room for misunderstanding." She added ruefully, "That's what was discovered by every one who became friendly with John Doyce."

"You were saying," said Slade, "that you found him attractive."

"I did. I shouldn't have married him unless I thought myself in love with him. I found out when it was too late that what I felt for John Doyce wasn't love. It wasn't anything deeper than a passing infatuation. But at the time I had little knowledge of the tricks one's emotions can play. Otherwise—"

She looked at Prines, and her glance softened.

"Yes, I would have married you, Peter, and saved myself years of unhappiness."

The photographer smiled at her.

"I'm ready to marry you any time you say, Lily. I've been wait-ing ever since you turned me down in favour of Doyce."

The woman's gaze met Slade's frankly.

"You see, Inspector," she said, "I was luckier than I deserved to be. I had two suitors. It was my misfortune that I chose to marry the wrong one. Poor Peter here wasn't so outwardly attractive, and I failed to read them aright. I married John Doyce. I think, Peter, you wanted to strangle me when I told you."

Prines got to his feet and pushed his hands into his trousers pockets.

"Strangle you, Lily? No. But I knew you were being a fool. I went home and told myself I too was a fool still to bother my head about you. But—there it was. I did. I said I'd see you through."

"And you did, Peter. You've been splendid, patient. Four years—"

Prines revealed just how much he cared for her by hurriedly covering a chink he saw in her armour.

"You see, Inspector," he explained, "Mrs Edwards has always had a horror of divorce courts. Her father divorced her mother when she was quite small. Well, I understood how she felt, and was prepared to wait," he added.

Slade found himself regarding this unusual couple afresh, trying to assess them in the light of these new values he had discovered.

"That was why you didn't divorce Doyce?"

"That was why, Inspector."

Slade nodded thoughtfully. "You say he asked you to marry him after Mary Kindilett's death?"

"Yes. The publicity of the inquest, and the way people talked—Ryechester had more than its share of scandalizing gossips, as Francis Kindilett found—and you found, too, didn't you, Peter?"

Prines gave her a quick smile, moved closer and patted her shoulder.

"Everything's going to be all right now, Lily dear," he assured her.

She returned his smile and then faced Slade again.

"I think her death shook him," she resumed. "Marriage suddenly offered an escape. From what? From what people were saying, from himself maybe. I don't know. Anyway, he asked me to marry him, and I was flattered. The life he held out was very tempting, as he pictured it. We were married. I suppose for a month—two months—we were happy. I was. Then it all crashed. I learned the truth about him. I suppose, with my home background, it hit me extra hard. It seemed to. I—I hated him. To give him his due, he wanted a divorce. He didn't mince words, and made no attempt to spare my feelings. He could be damnably candid. Perhaps that was the essence of his charm for so many women, his brutal candour about them. They felt themselves understood. Anyway, he told me he had made a mistake, that our marriage couldn't really mean anything to him, that he was the sort of man who shouldn't be married. I think he rather liked, at times, to paint himself in dark tones. It gave him a morbid satisfaction. A psychiatrist could probably give his particular complex a name. But I mustn't digress."

She paused to smooth her dress again. It was as though the action helped to smooth her thoughts also.

"He only became difficult when I told him I wouldn't divorce him. And I think he realized it was hopeless to expect a solution from the reverse procedure. He knew he wouldn't be given an opportunity," she added, her voice hardening perceptibly. "We had to compromise. Because I suddenly hated him I insisted upon receiving an allowance, and I came to London. I thought I could lose myself better in a large city. But you probably won't understand that."

"Indeed I do," Slade told her. "You have been here how long?"

"Nearly four years. It's seemed three times as long as that. I have a job. It doesn't pay me much. Otherwise I would have given up the allowance when I ceased hating him. Hate dies very quickly, you know."

This last was uttered in an introspective tone.

"You have not quarrelled recently?"

She looked up, eyes large and bright.

"Quarrelled?" The word surprised her. "No. Why should we? I became philosophic about my husband before I left Ryechester. But you, Peter"—she turned again to the photographer—"it's been difficult, hasn't it?"

Prines walked nearer to Slade. He took his hands from his pockets and folded his arms.

"I've been in love with Mrs Edwards, Inspector, since before she married Doyce. I am still in love with her. I think that gives me some—er—protective right."

He looked uncomfortable. Slade said nothing, waiting for what was to come.

"I think we should both like to know," Prines forced himself to continue, "why you are interested in her at this stage. She did not kill her husband. Surely, after four years of—"

His newly developed vehemence left him all but speechless.

"I am not suggesting Mrs Doyce killed her husband," said Slade coldly. "The fact remains that he was murdered. She may know something that will help us find the murderer."

The woman's gaze dropped.

"I was at the inquest," she said. "The coroner said that the police—"

She hesitated.

"We are still anxious to procure any fresh evidence," said Slade guardedly. "Evidence that would point to some one's hating your husband—enough to kill him."

"But, Inspector," said Prines, "you surely don't think—Why, I mean to say—"

"Did you hate him, Mr Prines?" asked the detective bluntly.

With an accusatory query directed at himself the man was more at ease than had it been directed against the woman.

"I could have killed him cheerfully—four years ago," he affirmed. "But four years is a long time, and, if she will pardon me, Mrs Edwards is an unusual woman. I have found her a great example. She has taught me patience and, I hope, fortitude."

It might have been pompous, but somehow it wasn't. There was a simplicity about the man's delivery that robbed his words of any sententiousness. Slade found this hard to credit. His every instinct was to suspect the man, yet the evidence of his eyes and ears confounded reason.

He stole a look at Clinton, and the knotted expression on the sergeant's face was proof that he was finding the situation as difficult to assess as was his chief.

"Peter didn't kill my husband," said the woman. "Nor did I. Both of us have read the papers. We can't prove we didn't send that package—or, at least, I can't. You were in Ryechester on Saturday, weren't you, Peter?"

"Yes. Had to make arrangements for photographing the wedding of a councillor's daughter. Elaborate show, but poor food," added the Society critic.

"And you were in London, Mrs Edwards," said Slade, conceding a point by using the name she was known by.

Her smile acknowledged the concession.

"Yes, I didn't go out till the afternoon, but as I live alone in this flat I can't prove that. But the papers said a man handed the package in at the District Messenger's office."

Slade caught Clinton's puzzled glance. The sergeant was stumped. It looked as though they were wasting their time by remaining. They had got nowhere, and their most hopeful lead had suddenly petered out.

"Why did you go to your husband's flat?" Slade pursued. "It would clear things considerably if I knew that."

For some seconds she remained silent. Prines took out a cigarette-case and absently lit a cigarette.

"Sorry," he said, turning to the others. "I was forgetting. Smoke?"

The Yard men declined, but the woman took a cigarette. As she lit it from Prines' match she sat back.

"I'll tell you. It was a stupid impulse, Inspector. As I told you, I was at the inquest this morning, and heard about the police being ready to wind up the case. That made me remember something."

She paused. The others waited, none offering any comment.

"I remembered that just after I was married my husband had a letter from Francis Kindilett. It was a very bitter letter. My husband told me he would keep it. One day, he said, it might come in handy. I don't know what he meant, exactly. But I did know he put that letter away. Whether he replied to it or not I can't say. But I thought perhaps the police haven't found it. I thought—Well, I saw Mr Kindilett's face at the inquest. He looked worried to death, and I suddenly made up my mind to get that letter, to avoid any misunderstanding. You see, the newspaper report about the investigation in Ryechester made it plain that the old tragedy was being brought out and aired again. And—" She broke off. "That's why I went to the flat."

"Did you find the letter?" asked Slade.

She shook her head.

"No," she said. "But I expect you know that. It occurred to me afterwards that I had acted hastily. The police would have been through my husband's correspondence already."

XV

After Office Hours

FROM A 'PHONE KIOSK AT THE CORNER OF CLIFFICKS GARDENS Slade rang up Morring's private address, and was lucky enough to find the footballer at home.

"I want to go through Doyce's desk at the office. Can you meet me there in half an hour?" the Yard man asked.

"Yes, certainly."

Slade went back to the car.

"He was in," he told Clinton. "He's meeting us at the office in half an hour. Got the address there?"

The sergeant again consulted his notebook containing names, addresses, and telephone numbers.

"Mallin's House, Peckbourne Street. That's in the City, off Moorgate."

Slade drove south, while the sergeant spoke his thoughts aloud.

"I don't think Prines is the sort to commit murder. Anyway, he wouldn't have waited all these years and then screwed up his courage, unless there had been a sudden development. And so far as we know there hasn't been. She didn't say there had. Funny, she should still be wearing her wedding-ring."

"No, I think that's consistent with her outlook. She felt bound to Doyce. She was his wife. Only death could alter that."

"Death has," Clinton ruminated. "Convenient for them. I suppose they'll get married somewhere in Town quietly and go back to face Ryechester. That'll take some pluck, if the gossips are as bad as she made out."

"She's got the pluck."

"And it would be asking too much for him to pull up his roots. He's doing pretty well just now."

"True. But he's very much in love with her. Not in a youthful, demonstrative way. He's the steady-flame type, Clinton, burns on and on. He'd throw up the Ryechester business if it would make her happy. Point is it wouldn't. Obviously she's been the one who has made sure he's kept pegging away where he had a chance of success. I don't think he'd be much without her. Four years ago he was running around snapping shots for the *Ryechester Chronicle*. Then she got married and the marriage went on the rocks. She cast adrift, and Prines started going ahead. Her work, as I see it."

Clinton digested this.

"Certainly looks that way, as you make it out. I wonder if he realizes it."

"I think so. What she says goes with him. Well, I wish them luck. They deserve a bit after waiting this long."

Clinton went off at a tangent.

"Queer, the way Doyce got himself tied up after the Kindilett girl's death. Must be something in it."

"As I see it," said Slade slowly, "Doyce broke up her engagement—"

"Mary Kindilett's?"

"Yes. I've mentioned this before. Now it looks fairly certain. He broke up her engagement out of what? Spite? Perhaps. Devilment? Perhaps. We don't know. But we know she went to that dance with him. Perhaps he was careless. Probably let slip something that told her the truth. That he had lied to her about her fiancé, and that tipped her emotions over."

"Which makes her death suicide."

"A suicide covered up as accidental death, Clinton, because her fiancé didn't come forward at the inquest and wash some private linen in public."

"But this letter from Kindilett?"

"Ah! That's a pointer. Her father suspected something, even if he didn't know the truth. He suspected Doyce's hand in the affair, and told him so. There must have been something pretty grim in that letter."

"Think we'll find it?"

"If the wife is right, he wouldn't have destroyed it. Imagine the position. Doyce joining Kindilett's new team, the Trojans, a team with a national reputation, and he had that letter hidden away. Of course, we don't know what's in it—yet. But the situation, as I see it, would appeal to Doyce's imagination. That letter might be a hold over Kindilett."

"That's rather changing things round, isn't it?"

"Yes. But we have Kindilett's official attitude towards Doyce to remember. He didn't bar him from the team. He just wasn't enthusiastic."

"But I don't see the point," said the sergeant. "How do you make anything out of that? What could Doyce have done?"

"It isn't what he could have done, Clinton, so much as what he knew."

Clinton grunted. "I don't want to become a blasted echo," he said, "but knew what?"

Slade swept round a bus and straightened the car.

"Every one we've questioned so far has told us he or she never knew the name of Mary Kindilett's fiancé. Even Kindilett falls into that line. He may be lying. I don't know. But if Doyce broke up that engagement, then obviously *he* knew who the girl's fiancé was. He could point to him, and he could talk. He could start gossip afresh about the girl's suicide. He could make Kindilett's life a fresh hell. Don't you see?"

"Yes, I missed that, I confess," said the sergeant. "But what satisfaction would it get him?"

Slade shrugged.

"Who can answer that now? We know Doyce made a mistake in marrying. Probably he has been cursing himself for that mistake ever since. It left him trammelled. He couldn't get a divorce. If he ever fell in love—if he could genuinely—he could do nothing about it. Mary Kindilett and her death would be, in his mind, directly responsible. Imagine the effect on him after four years of mulling it over. It could leave him mentally warped. I think it did. We saw the letters he had from women, and we know he kicked his heels up. It must have given him a very personal satisfaction at being back in Kindilett's life, knowing Kindilett resented him, as shown by that letter, and knowing further that he had the power—intangible, but nonetheless actual—of giving Kindilett pain."

"You're making him out to be a bit of a sadist."

"A man who plays about with women the way he did, stealing his partner's girl, probably for the fun of the thing, isn't he a sadist?"

Clinton grunted again. He saw the force of Slade's reasoning. It was psychological, rather than factual, but it added up. It produced a result. And that result was disturbingly far from the one Clinton himself had obtained earlier by linking facts to circumstances.

"All this builds up a stronger case not against Morring," he pointed out, "or even the unknown fiancé—but against Kindilett."

"That's the devil of it," said Slade. "It does. If we find that letter, and if its contents are what I think they are, and what Mrs Doyce knows they are, but wouldn't tell us, then Kindilett is in a spot."

"Hell! I shall want some aspirin if we keep this up," moaned Clinton.

Slade parked the car in a court near Mallin's House, a large, grey-stone building with massive bronze doors. The marble hall and staircase was taken over by an army of charwomen when the detectives arrived. They were bandying talk of the day as they swabbed and swept.

Slade and Clinton climbed to the second floor. Morring was waiting for them, standing inside an inner office, reading an evening paper. The windows were all closed, and there was a damp smell to the place that proclaimed the cleaners had done their work and passed on.

"Well, what is it you want here, Inspector?" asked the footballer.

"I want to go through Doyce's desk. I take it that it has been left untouched?"

"Yes. My time has been taken up with trying to straighten out his side of the business."

"Did it need—straightening?"

"Oh, don't misunderstand me, Inspector," said Morring quickly. "I merely meant that clients have been furiously ringing up wondering what is happening now they haven't him to look after their affairs. Apparently he left most of his people with the impression that no one else could look after them. That was rather in character, I'm afraid."

He showed the way into another office, small, compact, but comfortably furnished, with shelves containing files, and one or two water-colours on the walls.

"This was his office," Morring announced, switching on a desk-lamp.

"Was he married, do you know?"

The question was asked abruptly, and took the other completely by surprise.

"Married? Doyce? Good Lord, he'd be the last to get led to the altar! No, I can't see John Doyce in that meek role."

"Would it surprise you very much if I told you I have reason to believe he was married, nevertheless?"

Morring stared, and a slow smile, ironic, a trifle grim, twisted his mouth.

"Surprise me? It would amaze me, Inspector. If some one told you that they've been pulling your leg—hard."

"Think so?" Slade smiled back.

"Certain of it."

There remained no doubt in the other's mind; that much was patent.

"Did you come to find something in particular?" Morring inquired after a pause.

"Yes, a letter." Slade gestured to Clinton, who started searching the desk, making a thorough job of it. "A letter," he enlarged, "that Doyce received shortly after Mary Kindilett's death."

"Oh. Know what was in it?"

"No. But I believe I know who wrote it."

Morring's smile, which had receded, returned in full. "You'd have difficulty recognizing it if you didn't know who wrote it, wouldn't you?" he asked dryly.

"Depends. Some letters aren't signed," Slade reminded him. "Some letter-writers deem it safer not to add their name."

"I see. One of that sort."

"I don't know. Possibly. That's all."

Slade joined the sergeant in his search. Morring stood by, smoking, and occasionally dropping a conversational word. But neither Yard man appeared willing to divert his attention from the work in hand.

The desk produced nothing save a mass of business and personal correspondence of no interest to the detectives. Clinton turned to the shelves as Slade tidied the desk and put the loose sheets away in their several drawers. The files on the shelves, however, produced nothing after twenty minutes' careful scrutiny and thorough sifting. Morring was smoking his third cigarette and had desisted from trying to make conversation by the time the sergeant came to the end of the last shelf and announced a negative result.

"Nothing here. Maybe," he hinted darkly, "our leg was being pulled."

Slade did not rise to the bait. He was going through a file cabinet standing in one corner of the office. It had been locked, but a key on the bunch he carried with him had opened it. The lowest tray of the cabinet had been at some time removed, leaving a deep well in the bottom. In the well was a black japanned box. Slade took out the box and stood it on the desk. It had the white initials "J.D." painted on the lid.

"Hallo," said Morring, with new interest, "I haven't seen that box before. It's a new one on me."

Slade's bunch produced another key, which unlocked the box. Inside was an assortment of papers, most of them secured with rubber bands.

The first pile were personal insurance policies.

Morring frowned. "These weren't put through the office," he complained, as though he had discovered an irregularity in procedure.

Slade had thrown the bundle of policies on to the desk, and was fingering the next pile. The papers appeared to be, for the most part, figures detailing a betting system, but whether it had ever been tried out, and whether, if tried out, it had been successful or a failure, he had no means of telling.

"H'm. Close secrets. He probably thought they were safer here than at his flat."

"Fewer females to pry here," said Morring sardonically.

Clinton strolled over, and watched them. He saw Slade pick up a folded sheet of paper from the black box and open it out, and he saw Slade's face light as he read the first words.

"Got it?" he asked.

"Yes. This is it, Clinton."

There was a quiet triumph in Slade's tone, but he said no more as his eyes ran down the page of neat, compact writing. The light vanished from his face. When he had finished reading he passed the letter to Clinton. Morring, looking from one man to the other, moved to the sergeant's side and peered over his shoulder.

The letter ran:

> "I think you know, from what I said to you after the inquest on Friday last, that I hold you morally responsible for Mary's death. The truth did not come out at the inquiry. You and I know that. I believe you deliberately wrecked my daughter's life, and for that I shall never be able to forgive you. I believe

you will have this on your conscience for the rest of your life.
May it weigh heavily. For myself, I can only say I consider you
a blackguard, and were I a younger man I should ask nothing
more than an opportunity to break your neck. It would be
better for both of us if we did not meet again."

Beneath this was a small, neat signature, "Francis J. Kindilett."

"Well, this sticks a label on the can," said Clinton, handing the letter back to Slade.

Morring was a man stunned.

"How did you know such a letter existed?" he asked. "It is news to me. I never—"

"Did you expect Doyce to show it to you?" said Slade.

"No, but—" Morring shook his head. "This—I mean it is awful. After what has happened…"

"Exactly," said Slade grimly. "After what has happened it reads very interestingly."

"But good God, man! You can't imagine for a moment that Kindilett murdered Doyce."

Slade studied the other. Morring's face was in half-shadow, the light from the desk-lamp only touching one side of it.

"He left Ryechester soon after his daughter's death. So far as I can find out, he and Doyce did not meet again until your partner joined the Trojans. Right?"

"Yes, I suppose so," Morring admitted reluctantly. He looked troubled, and made no attempt to hide his disturbed feelings.

"And that was only a matter of a few days ago. Doyce is murdered during his first match with the team. It would seem to make a piece."

"But it's preposterous, unthinkable—"

"Preposterous?" Slade shrugged. "Read the evidence of most murder trials which result in a verdict of guilty. Most of it is preposterous. Because a great deal of human behaviour *is* preposterous, but we rarely confess the fact. But unthinkable? No. Read the letter through again. I should say that, four years ago, Kindilett thought very much along these lines. He cleared out of Ryechester—"

"Because of gossip, because the situation was intolerable, and because—well, he couldn't live there—"

"True enough. But are you sure it was entirely on account of gossip that he cleared out?" Slade persisted. "He is a man with very strong powers of endurance. He is dogged. Best testimony to those qualities is the team you belong to. He fought hard, against considerable odds, to make that team. He wasn't easily put off."

Morring's clenched fist smote the desk.

"What are you driving at?" he demanded.

Slade held up the letter.

"Mind if I keep this?"

"No," snapped Morring.

"Right." The letter disappeared into the detective's wallet. He answered the question that had been put to him. "I'm not driving at anything. I'm just trying to show that this letter would be considered as vital evidence by a prosecution counsel."

"What was written four years ago in a moment of heat can't rightly be considered as applicable to-day, after all this time."

Morring seemed determined to defend the absent man. His very determination interested Slade.

"Taken by itself, no, I agree," said the detective slowly. "But circumstances give it point. The circumstances of Doyce's entry into the team—an entry you yourself contended—"

"But that was not so much on personal grounds."

"Are you sure?"

"Well—"

"You obviously aren't sure. You feel that personal feelings might have weighed with you. That's only natural. All right. How about Kindilett? Couldn't personal feelings have weighed with him too? And more strongly than in your case? After all—"

"Oh, don't go on with it!" Morring cried, turning away from the desk. "The more one chews it over the—the more nauseating it is. I can't believe Kindilett murdered him. But I see now what was meant by the coroner this morning. This is what you expected to find."

Slade did not correct him. He glanced at Clinton. There was a sardonic grin on the sergeant's face. The situation, with its peculiar dramatic values, its protestations and personal comparisons, appealed to his sanely cynical mind. As he had told Slade more than once in the past, a murderer who doesn't lie and deceive to cover up his guilt is a fool. A man's neck is worth a string of lies. Slade wondered just what Clinton was making of things now. His case against Morring, the latter's defence of Kindilett in view of this letter, which, as a piece of possible court-room evidence, was a bombshell.

A charwoman's voice rang through the offices.

"Hey, Doris, what did you do with my other brush?"

"Well," said Slade, "I think we've finished here now. There's nothing else we want."

A mocking smile touched Morring's lips.

"You seem suddenly sure, Inspector."

Slade was putting the rubber-banded bundles back in the japanned box.

"Later," he said, ignoring the other's comment, "I shall want your partner's pass-book. He didn't happen to mention a Mrs Edwards to you, did he?"

"Edwards? No, I don't recall the name. Was she a client, do you think?"

"Well, not in the customary sense."

A grunt came from Clinton. Morring glanced at the sergeant.

"I see," he said. "Like that. No, I don't know the name at all. Is that everything, Inspector?"

His tone was somewhat more distant, reserved.

"I think so, for the time being," said Slade easily. "Oh, you might tell me if you knew a pub in Ryechester called the Fox and Ferret."

"Yes. Best place for a drink of beer in the town."

"You patronized it?"

"I'm not what might be called a drinking man. But I went into the Fox and Ferret occasionally. Why?"

"Don't happen to remember a barmaid there called Lily, do you?"

"I don't see the point of all this," said Morring, "but as it happens I do remember her. She stuck out a mile above the other barmaids. To forestall your next question, Inspector, I'll tell you at once, she was a very superior girl, and I believe the laddie who used to take group photos of the team was stuck on her."

"Prines?"

"That might have been his name. I don't remember. I was never interested in him. And now, what the devil does this all mean?"

"It means," said Slade, with a smile, "that you've been most helpful. Sorry if I can't be more explicit in return. And now we won't keep you any longer."

XVI

Highbury Nocturne

I T WAS AFTER EIGHT O'CLOCK WHEN SLADE LEFT THE A.C.'S room at Scotland Yard and returned to the office of Department X2. Clinton had gone. Taking out his pipe, the detective filled and lit it, and for a quarter of an hour smoked reflectively. He had had a long day following previous long days, but he was not tired. He felt intensely alive, as a matter of fact. Things were clearing themselves in his mind. The A.C. had gone over the case with the Commissioner, and both were convinced that the strongest case was against Morring. There had been a sharp reminder from the A.C. that a result was expected very shortly. Slade had been granted his extension of time to complete his search for evidence, the inquest had been adjourned, and now the Press was waiting for something that would show the Yard knew their business. To-morrow was Wednesday. A move—a definite move—was expected.

Slade had received the intimation that it was now up to him.

Going over what the day had produced, assessing it in the light of what he had previously uncovered, Slade found himself in two minds. The case against Morring remained strong, although he personally was still convinced that the footballer was innocent. The case he had constructed against Kindilett was not so strong at first viewing, but it was fundamentally sound theory, built up from a wide, firm base of fact. Yet Slade was not content. Out of the evidence he had procured there should be something that would clarify the issue in his mind.

He had yet to produce the murder "weapon," which he was convinced was a solitaire engagement ring that had once been on Mary Kindilett's left hand. Could he use that object to precipitate his solution? Could he combine it with the effect produced at the inquest that morning to force the murderer's hand? Bring him into the open?

Possibilities, suggestions, the vague outline of new theories passed through his mind, a progressive array of phantoms that somehow eluded his mental grasp.

He felt restive. He had an urge to follow this Kindilett theory to its ultimate conclusion. He wanted to *know*.

He picked up the 'phone.

"Get me George Allison's home," he told the operator.

A couple of minutes later he was speaking to the Arsenal manager.

"I'm doing nothing more important than reading a Western novel," said Allison. "Come round by all means, Inspector."

For the second time that day Slade drove north through London, this time to Golders Green. He drew up before a house fronted by a row of neatly trimmed trees. The maid who answered his ring said, "Mr Allison is expecting you, sir."

The Arsenal manager rose from the depths of an easy-chair.

"You chose a night when the rest of the family are out," he smiled.

"Then I'm not interrupting—"

Allison waved a hand. "Just this horse-opera, I believed it's called. As a matter of fact, Western fiction is one of my weaknesses. Two-gun men, bad sheriffs, tough hombres, and all the rest of it. Oh, and I was trying out this radio of mine. It's an old friend that's suddenly gone back on me."

He pointed to a small wireless set on a side-table.

"I bought it in America years ago, and it travels around with me. It's just recently started to protest. But—a drink?"

Slade found himself supplied with a glass of whisky and a cigarette.

It was a comfortable room with soft lighting reflected from pale-coloured walls. The cool note of a green silk suite contrasted with the warm gleam of oranges piled in a crystal basket. The brightness of daffodils enlivened the sheen of natural oak.

Allison turned back from a cocktail cabinet and raised his glass.

"Well, here's luck, Inspector."

They drank.

"Excuse me," said Allison, attentive as a host.

An ash-tray decorated with a pheasant in bright colours was put at Slade's elbow.

It was as though both men were reluctant to allow a grim reality to intrude into an atmosphere of peace and tranquillity. They sipped their drinks, smoked, chatted for some minutes about sport in its general aspects, before Slade said, "I really came to talk about Kindilett."

Allison nodded.

"I see."

Slade studied the man opposite him. Small in height, with full figure, Allison had a fighter's jaw and a pair of shrewd eyes shadowed by jutting brows. There was strength in the face, Slade saw, and humour. The quick smile that came to the firm mouth indicated a ready understanding. A man who could see both sides of a question and remain with a mind of his own.

"How can I help you, Inspector?"

The question was typical of the man and his methods, to the point, leading somewhere.

"I want to see Kindilett from a friend's perspective, Mr Allison. I want to know his qualities, what he's capable of."

"You think I can tell you?"

Allison's gaze was thoughtful, his jaw squared.

"I do," said Slade bluntly. "When I spoke to him I came up against a barrier. I can't quite explain it, but I was conscious of it, a barrier of reserve. We both tried to pretend it wasn't there, but we both knew it was. I think it was this reserve that tended to make him—well, suspicious."

Allison leaned forward, put down his glass.

"It isn't just suspicion, Inspector, if you'll allow me. Francis is an old friend of mine, as I've already told you. I've known him for years. He's been a man with a dream, but not a dreamer. You'll appreciate the difference."

Slade nodded. "He wanted to put amateur football in England back on its one-time high pedestal."

"Exactly," Allison said. "He worked damned hard, and he succeeded. That's as the world sees him, as the Press reports him. But his friends know he is a man with a broken heart. I'm being very frank."

There was a pause, till Slade said, "You agree, then, that he never fully recovered from his daughter's death?"

"I know he didn't," said Allison. "Could he be expected to?"

"I suppose not. But to be personal for a moment, Mr Allison, how do you think he's taken this business of Doyce?"

"Hard—damned hard," said the Arsenal manager convincingly. "I was speaking to him to-day, after the inquest. He's terribly cut up. That report about the investigation in Ryechester—it's open-ing old wounds."

Slade realized that Allison was utterly sincere in what he said. He was speaking about a man he admired, for whom he enter-tained real friendship and genuine sympathy.

But Slade was outside that orbit of friendship. He could ask himself—was Allison right?

Kindilett had told him that his daughter had worn a solitaire engagement ring for two days. It had suddenly disappeared from her hand. Obviously she had quarrelled with her fiancé, and pre-sumably had given back the ring. And Slade was positive of one thing; every piece of deductive reasoning pointed to it. Namely, the ring which had brought death to John Doyce was the solitaire ring Mary Kindilett had worn.

Hence the Press cutting. Hence the poison, the pricked enve-lope. A prised-up claw smeared with aconitine. Was it adding a gesture to murder? A reminder of the past?

Then, again, supposing Mary Kindilett had not given back her ring. Supposing her father had later found it in her room, and had kept it...

"Something's puzzling you, Inspector," said Allison, studying the Yard man's face. "Have another drink. It'll help."

He rose and refilled their glasses.

"Cigarette?"

"No, thanks, I'll try my pipe."

The Arsenal manager returned to his chair. "I'd like to ask you something, Inspector."

"Go ahead," Slade invited.

"Are you seriously considering Francis Kindilett as a—a suspect?"

Slade drew on his pipe, tamped the ash in the bowl with his little finger.

"I've got to. But there are features that leave me undecided. Would you care to hear the facts?"

Slade asked the question with knowledge of the man to whom he was putting it. Had Allison considered himself in no fair position to advise the Yard man, had he not, in effect, been able to listen with an open mind, he would have said no.

Instead, he said, "I should, very much," and Slade knew that, whatever the ties of friendship, George Allison could still remain honest and impartial in his judgment.

"Very well. Briefly, they are these."

He gave the Arsenal manager in outline the facts that made a case against Kindilett. He told him of the letter, but omitted to mention Doyce's wife. For the first time he showed Allison the Press cutting and the report in the *Ryechester Chronicle*.

Allison sat silent, attentive, impressed visibly. He said nothing until Slade showed him the photograph, which he studied closely before glancing up.

"By the way, I've got an album Francis loaned me. Would you care to see it? It's filled with football photos of different kinds. There are quite a few of the Saxon Rovers team of four years ago."

"Thanks, I should very much."

Allison rose and went out of the room. To Slade it seemed significant that the Arsenal manager had made no comment on the array of facts that he had presented.

Allison came back, carrying a large-sized volume bound in grey morocco. He placed it on the centre table, and Slade rose and opened it. He turned over the grey-green pages, glancing at the photographs fixed by their corners.

But there was none that interested him except one showing a group of footballers in quartered shirts and light knickers. Among them was the man with the moustache who was in the photograph he had brought from Ryechester.

He slipped the photograph out of its page and turned it over. On the back in pencil was written, in a handwriting he recognized as the same as that in the letter to Doyce: "Some of the Saxon Amateurs—1935."

"Do you recognize any of them?" he asked Allison.

Allison studied the group, but shook his head.

"No, I'm afraid I don't, Inspector."

Slade replaced the photograph in the album and handed the volume back to the other.

"There's one thing I've still to find, Mr Allison," he confided.

The Arsenal manager gave him a sharp glance.

"I can guess what that is, Inspector. The object that pricked Doyce's thumb."

"Yes—exactly. I'm convinced that object—as you might have gathered from what I've told you—is a solitaire diamond engagement ring."

"Mary Kindilett's—"

"That's what I believe."

"And you think you'll find it?"

"I'm certain it is somewhere in the Stadium."

Allison started. Whatever he had been expecting, this had come as a surprise.

"Good Lord! You really think that?"

Slade nodded. "I feel certain the murderer took the ring from Doyce's clothes after the team had gone on to the field for the second half."

"That lets out one obvious suspect, then—Morring," said Allison quickly. "Possibly Setchley too. And Francis himself. But doesn't that let out the whole team? I—" George Allison paused, genuinely stumped. "I begin to see something of what you're up against, Inspector. Might I ask what you have in mind? You had some real reason"—Allison smiled wryly—"in coming to see me."

Slade nodded. "I'd like to go over the dressing-rooms and treatment room again," he said. "Preferably with yourself."

"Of course. But when?"

"Now," Slade said, "to-night."

If Allison was surprised again, at this request, he managed successfully to keep his surprise to himself. He was a man well able to produce action when necessary. He pushed Kindilett's album across the table, picked up the detective's glass, and said, "Another drink, and I'm your man, Inspector."

Ten minutes later Slade and Allison were heading for Highbury.

"It's a bit fortunate that you chose Tuesday night," the Arsenal manager explained as the car left Golders Green behind. "Bernard Joy, our centre-half, trains at the Stadium on Tuesday and Thursday evenings. He's a schoolmaster, but has to get in his training. Whittaker generally comes with him one night in the week, Milne, the assistant-trainer, the other."

"They're still here," Slade remarked when he drew into the kerb before the Arsenal Stadium gates. A light shone in the hall.

He followed Allison into the building. There was an eerie atmosphere about the deserted Stadium. It might have been the entrance hall of a museum in which Slade stood—until Allison pushed open the swing door leading to the dressing-rooms. From farther along the corridor came *The Chestnut Tree* whistled off-key.

"Here's the visitors' dressing-room," said Allison, opening a door and switching on a light. "If you'll excuse me, Inspector, I'll just have a word with Whittaker while I'm here."

He left Slade to begin a thorough search of the tiled apartment. But the detective, as he had expected, met with no success in that room. There were few places where anything could be hidden. He went into the bathroom beyond.

He was methodically feeling round the baths when padding feet sounded behind him. He turned, to meet the interested gaze of a tall, fair-haired man with fresh complexion. Bernard Joy was rubbing his head with a towel.

"I don't need to inquire if you're looking for something," he smiled.

"I'm not having much success," Slade told him.

"Something little?" The towel went on rubbing the tousled head.

Slade straightened. An idea had just occurred to him.

"If you had to hide something, Joy," he said, "something dangerous and smaller round than, say, a halfpenny—where would you conceal it?"

Bernard Joy continued wiping his left ear while the fingers of his right hand meditatively scratched his bare chest.

"You mean in this bathroom?"

"No, not necessarily," said Slade, in the tone of some one expounding a problem. "But somewhere in either this room, the dressing-room next to this, the treatment room, or—no, you can leave out the Arsenal players' dressing-room and bathroom—"

"That leaves the visitors' rooms and treatment room—and, yes, Tom's office?"

"Right. But you've got to put this something where it won't be seen. Probably where it won't be looked for. Somewhere, too, where you can recover it when you want it."

Bernard Joy regarded the detective thoughtfully.

"You're serious in this, Inspector?"

"Absolutely."

The towel recommenced its vigorous rubbing, bringing a pink flush to the fair man's skin.

"I know a bit about schoolboys' capers, but—The treatment room's sealed."

"That doesn't matter. We can break the seals."

"In that case, that's where I'd look. If I was hiding this object you speak of, and wanted to do it effectively and quickly, I'd choose somewhere in that large glass cabinet with its shelves of bottles." Bernard Joy slung the towel round his neck and folded his arms. "A boy in class can usually get away with something he conceals under the master's nose. It's something hidden at a distance, given perspective as it were, that is quickly found."

"My own idea," Slade said.

At that moment George Allison returned.

"Oh, there you are, Joy. Whittaker wants to give that arm another run over. Can't be too careful, and we've got a hard away game on Saturday."

Joy nodded. "Tom's a bit worried, but it's going along nicely. I've been resting it. Well, happy hunting," he threw cheerfully at Slade, "even if I don't know what it's all about."

"Drawn a blank?" asked Allison as the centre-half went through the door.

"In here—yes. But I only covered these visitors' rooms as a kind of preliminary routine."

"Then you think it's in the treatment room?"

"I do."

Allison fingered his chin.

"That means whoever took the ring carried it on the field of play with him during the second half."

"No, I don't think so."

Allison looked puzzled. "McEwan and the commissionaire established that no one came along the corridor," he pointed out, revealing to the detective that he had followed the established evidence closely.

"True enough," Slade agreed. "But there was an interval after the match, before you locked the doors and 'phoned the Yard. There was opportunity then for some one to conceal the ring in the treatment room, and people were probably drifting in and out."

Allison looked grave.

"That's true, Inspector. I was forgetting. But surely if the ring was hidden then—well, anyone could have done it?"

"Yes, the issue is widened considerably. The only narrowing down one can do is from motive pure and simple."

"Always supposing it was that ring," put in Allison shrewdly.

"Yes, always supposing that," Slade agreed.

Slade broke the seal on the door of the treatment room that led into Whittaker's small office. He unlocked the door, and followed by the Arsenal manager he entered the room where John Doyce had breathed his last, and which had been shut up since the two Yard men had left it on the Saturday.

The photographs and finger-prints taken by Irvin had not proved of any material assistance, but Slade was still careful not to disturb surface conditions as he moved around. Allison lit a cigarette and stood with hands in the pockets of his overcoat, watching the detective.

Slade crossed to one of the sun-ray machines, switched it on, and examined its interior through a pair of smoked glasses which he took from a rack. He switched off the machine and removed the goggles from his face.

"There was just a chance it might have been poked away inside one of these," he explained, pointing to the machines.

Allison nodded. He watched Slade examine the other sun-ray machines without comment. But the Yard man finished his examination without finding anything. He turned to the sink, went from that to the wall-racks and the cupboards. He was very thorough, and he did not hurry his search. Finally he turned to the large case of bottles and jars containing various medical supplies.

"Fitted out like a hospital," he said.

"We've got to be," said Allison.

Slade went to work on the shelves of bottles containing liquids of all colours. As he removed the jars—holding each with his hand-kerchief—took out the stoppers, and peered inside the atmosphere became heavy with the tang of ammonia and turpentine and of the various patent embrocations and liniments.

This was the slowest task of all. George Allison leaned against one of the treatment tables and lit fresh cigarettes.

The minutes dragged by. Bernard Joy pushed his head round the door to wish the two men good-night. Then Whittaker came and held a whispered conversation with Allison about the team. They stood together, smoking, for some minutes, watching the Yard man. Whittaker called good-night, left, and Allison returned to the treatment table.

"Slow work, Inspector," he said.

"Looking for a needle in a haystack always is," said Slade, straightening his back. "Not many years ago an American tried to find the answer to that stock problem. It took him some eighty-odd hours, working steadily."

"Feel like a rest?"

"No, I'll finish it while I'm at it."

Slade picked up the next bottle, unstoppered it, looked inside, swirled the blue liquid round, held it up to the light, and shook his head.

"No luck," he muttered.

He continued along the shelf, moved down to the next. But he did not find what he sought. He was feeling very tired, and his back ached when he bent over a glass dish with a grubby label on which the words "Sterilized horsehair" were printed in ink. He removed the glass lid, and held the dish up to the light.

Inside was a mauve liquid covering dark coils of hair thread. Peering down into the dish, Slade saw nothing save the coloured spirit and the dark hair coils. But when he shook the dish, moving the hair coils, and held the dish again to the light, he caught a momentary flash of tiny fires.

He picked up a pair of tweezers from a glass-topped table, and prodded among the horsehair.

"Found it?" queried Allison, unable to control the excitement in his voice.

"I think so," said Slade. "Yes—I have," he added, putting down the dish and holding up the tweezers for Allison's inspection.

Held in the narrow jaws of the tweezers was a solitaire diamond ring. One claw was prised up.

Allison took a deep breath.

"So you were right, Inspector," he murmured, and there was a sad note in his voice. "I was hoping you were wrong—utterly wrong." He peered closer at the exhibit, then stood back. "What does it mean?" he asked, pointing to the ring. "Have you completed your case?"

Slade put the ring on the table, replaced the dish of sterilized horsehair.

"Not quite. I shall have some thinking to do between now and to-morrow, when the players arrive for training. With the inquest this morning, they missed a day."

"Yes, but what have you in mind?"

Allison appeared suddenly anxious. There might be some hazard in the final catching of the murderer. And at the back of his mind was the rather pathetic figure of his friend Francis Kindilett.

Slade produced a stout manilla envelope, dropped the ring in it, folded the envelope carefully, and wrapped it in his handkerchief. After he had safely stowed the package in his overcoat pocket he turned again to the Arsenal manager.

"What have I in mind?" he repeated, an unusual abstraction in his manner. "Well, I don't rightly know. I had an idea when the coroner—" He hesitated, shook his head as though to clear it. "I've got to make the murderer show his hand," he said grimly, his manner again decisive.

"You think the coroner's intimation that the police were on to something will work?"

"I'm hoping so. But I see now there's got to be something else. If the murderer is less sure of himself to-night, because of what the coroner said, and because this place has been closed to him for a day, then advantage must be taken of the change. This man has been very sure of himself all along. He's been clever."

"You know his… identity?"

Allison's eyes bored into the Yard man's face.

Slade nodded slowly.

"I think so—now."

"You mean, after finding the ring, the case fits together, and—"

Slade was shaking his head.

"No, I think I made my mind up in your drawing-room, Mr Allison. If I'm right, if it works out the way I think it will, then I've to thank you for showing me the way to solve the case."

"Me?" Allison looked surprised. "But I don't remember saying anything that would—"

"It wasn't so much what you said, as what you did," smiled Slade, but his smile was tired. "Now, shall we call it a day, and sleep over what we've found?"

XVII

A Pair of Stained Hands

CLINTON WAS AT THE YARD BEFORE SLADE THE NEXT MORN-
ing. The sergeant greeted his superior with a glum, "I haven't
slept a wink. Your 'phone call last night kept me awake, puzzling
over the whole darned case."

"And what did the puzzling produce?" asked Slade.

"That's the devil of it. Nothing," Clinton grumbled. "Nothing
that we haven't already gone over and chopped up, and—"

He eyed Slade thoughtfully.

"You don't think Morring did it now," he said.

"I didn't think Morring guilty—"

"I know," Clinton interposed quickly. "What I mean is, *now*,
with the ring, you don't think it possible for him to have killed
his partner."

It wasn't a question. It was a statement.

"No, I don't. Unless he was Mary Kindilett's fiancé, and unless
she returned the ring to him."

Clinton screwed up his face.

"Even that doesn't make a good case—now," he said pointedly.

"It makes a very poor case," Slade agreed. "One can shoot it
full of holes without taking aim. For instance, why did he become
the partner of the man who stole his girl? Why wait four years?

Because of what was happening between Doyce and the Laruce girl? Not a bit of it. Morring's out now—clear."

Clinton continued to gloom.

"That leaves us with—"

He paused hopefully.

Slade smiled. "I think I'm right, Clinton, but I may be wrong. If I'm not wrong I'll get our man with all the evidence we want."

"After he's been so smart?"

"Curiosity plus self-preservation plus a strong measure of sentiment—that's the potion we're going to brew, Clinton. And it's got to do the trick for us."

Slade got out of his seat, where he had been toying with some papers, and began pacing the office. He glanced at his watch.

"We'll let the others get to the Stadium first. I want the atmosphere neutral when we arrive."

Clinton sat watching him. It was only at very infrequent intervals that Slade showed any sign of nervous strain. But the signs were apparent now. Clinton, who alone knew, besides Slade himself, how long the other had spent on the case, the hours with little sleep, the constant accumulating of facts, the probing, the recasting, the preparation of reports, guessed that his superior was physically tired out. It was a strange spiritual strength that kept the man going.

Clinton himself had his patch of garden to relax in—when he could get to it. Slade's life was cast in a different mould. Success had brought its surest reward, more work. There was no relaxation for Slade except the annual holiday.

"I don't think you slept much yourself last night," said the sergeant.

Slade looked up.

"Do I look it?"

"No, but I can tell."

Slade nodded. "I didn't turn in till past four. I was seeing how it all worked out on paper. When I tried to sleep I started thinking it all out again in the dark."

"It did work out?" asked Clinton, seizing on the one essential.

Slade nodded. "Yes, one thing was missing."

"Only one?"

"That I could see. A visit to a chemist's. I've made the visit. Now everything's ready."

Clinton didn't pretend to understand. He was about to ask another question when the house 'phone rang. He picked up the receiver, listened.

"Yes, sir," he said, and put down the receiver.

"The A.C. He's in already, and wants to see you," he told Slade.

"I rather thought he would." Slade paused at the door. "Be ready by the time I get back. We'll go straight off to Highbury."

The A.C. nodded good-morning. His manner was brisk, and he came straight to the point.

"Well, have you got your case straightened out now, Slade?"

Slade knew his man. He didn't say, "I think so." He said, "Yes."

A glint came to the A.C.'s eyes.

"Good. It'll stand up without props?"

"It will when I come back—with the prisoner."

"Morring?"

Slade shook his head.

"No, he's out."

"Then you were right?"

"I found the murder object last night. It's at the laboratory now, being tested for aconitine. I thought it best to waste no time—"

"Quite right."

"And there is a chance they can let me have a report before I actually make the arrest. I'd like that, if time allows."

"Why, any doubts?"

"No, not doubts. But I like having everything positive, no loose ends—just in case."

The A.C. nodded over his desk. "I understand. Good. Now let's hear some of it."

Slade spoke for a quarter of an hour. When he had finished the A.C. picked up a pencil and began revolving it between finger and thumb.

"There's an element of risk," he muttered.

"But if it comes off," Slade pointed out, "we've got something as good as a confession. Perhaps the confession will follow."

A slow smile broke on the A.C.'s face. He dropped the pencil and stood up.

"All right, take it in your own stride, Slade. And for all our sakes I hope you're right. I won't keep you any longer now."

Slade went back to his own office. Clinton was sitting in his coat and hat. Slade slipped into his outdoor clothes, and they left. They arrived at the Arsenal Stadium about half-past ten. The morning's training and practice was well under way.

Allison was awaiting the Yard men in his room.

"All set?" he asked. The look of strain was still on his face.

"Yes," said Slade. "I saw Whittaker just now and had a word with him. There's something I want him to do for me. You didn't mind?"

"Not at all, Inspector. Go right ahead, and do what you want to."

"Is Kindilett on the training-ground?"

"Yes. Want him brought up?"

"No, thanks. I'll slip downstairs for a few minutes. Shan't be long."

Slade went out. Allison pushed a box of cigarettes towards Clinton.

"Smoke, sergeant?"

"No, thanks."

Clinton didn't feel like relaxing. He didn't know what Slade was up to, but he did know, from long years of close working with his superior, that Slade had determined his course of action and he would go through with it.

"Come prepared to make an arrest?" asked the Arsenal manager.

"That's the general idea," said the sergeant.

"Can't say I like this waiting period," Allison confessed. "The lull before the storm."

Clinton nodded.

"Nor me."

Allison gave him a sharp glance, and his brows shot up.

"But you know—who!" he said.

Clinton leaned back in his chair, crossed one leg over the other, and folded his arms.

"You'd think it. Anybody'd think it," he said, nodding his head. "But I don't. The A.C. himself don't know for sure, if I don't miss a guess. The Inspector always runs his own cases. He always gets his man, too," said Clinton, with full pride. "Anyway, I've never known him fall down on a case."

"That's a great record," said Allison, to whom this news afforded a sense of boding disaster. "You think the law of averages will work in this case, too, eh?"

Clinton lifted his gaze.

"If you mean do I think he'll get the right man—yes, I haven't any doubt. Nor much idea," he added, on a note of morose frankness.

"But surely you've seen all the evidence—I mean, sergeant, you have *some* idea."

Allison wasn't idly probing the other man; his words were coloured by the unhappy state of his thoughts. He could visualize his friend Francis Kindilett arrested as a murderer, and he knew the far-reaching effect that conclusion of the case would have. Amateur sport throughout the country would receive a definite set-back. At the moment Kindilett was looked up to as a man who had persevered and produced something worth-while. A man who had shown what amateurs in sport could achieve.

Were that man hanged as a murderer...

"Sure, I had *some* idea." Clinton's words dragged the Arsenal manager back from the gloom of his own speculation. "To be frank, I thought it was Morring. Everything pointed to him. The Inspector said that made the case against him weak. It was too tight. It would have to crack somewhere."

"Did it?" asked Allison, as the other man paused.

"Did it!" Clinton sounded disgusted. "How the hell can that ring have anything to do with Morring? Had he been engaged to Mary Kindilett we wouldn't have had to wait four years."

"And you've no substitute for Morring?"

Clinton's eyes narrowed.

"Officially—no. I'm sitting on the fence. I know it's no good doing anything else. The Inspector's got it doped out. He'll provide the answer, and it'll be the right one, I know that. But, speaking personally, I've an idea—yes, and I may not be so far out at that."

With dramatic instinct Clinton paused.

"And that idea, sergeant?"

Allison leaned forward, stubbed out his cigarette.

Clinton unfolded his arms, rubbed his jaw,

"Kindilett—the girl's father. It's only my personal theory, as it were, but that's the only substitute I can find for Morring. The case fits him, and he fits the case."

"But the ring?" queried Allison.

Clinton wrinkled his nose.

"She left it at home, and he found it after her death. Kept it, and after Doyce joined the club—"

He shrugged.

"Kindilett says the ring just disappeared."

Clinton looked very straight at the Arsenal manager.

"If you had killed a man, Mr Allison, and wanted to cover up your tracks, and a simple lie would seem the best way of covering them up—wouldn't you tell that lie?"

Allison acknowledged the shrewdness of the question by not answering it.

Clinton, fearing that he might not be understood, was quick to add, "Of course, I didn't mean you personally, Mr Allison. I was speaking in general, you understand."

"I understand," said Allison heavily.

He did, only too well. Clinton's words had shown him the way official contemplation had possibly developed. And there was something about the sergeant's manner—his easy gesture and detachment—that made Allison feel the words were not founded upon any loose or unsound construction.

"You think there's a chance that is Inspector Slade's theory?"

Again Clinton shrugged.

"Might be. Again, it might not. I can't tell. He is the only one that knows his own business, and he won't tell till he's ready."

As though the words were a cue for his reappearance, Slade opened the door and entered before Allison could say anything further.

"That's that," he announced, without bothering to add an explanation.

"And now?" asked Allison.

"Now," said Slade, "I think we'll wait for half an hour or so."

Allison evinced surprise.

"Just—wait? For half an hour?"

"Yes. I think that'll be long enough," said Slade, with maddening placidity.

There was a rap on the door. Whittaker appeared.

"You've fixed that for me?" asked Slade.

"Yes," the trainer nodded. A twinkle of amusement was apparent in his bright eyes. "There was a bit of chaff from some of the boys, but the rumour's going round."

"Fine. Thanks a lot," said Slade.

Whittaker glanced at Allison, who sat silent, and after a nod to Clinton went out and closed the door.

"So you've started a rumour," said Allison.

"Of a sort," Slade confessed. "First I got Whittaker to see that the players' corridor is left deserted. He's got all the players outside."

"Arsenal and Trojans?"

"Yes, both. I also got him to spread the news that the treatment room is now opened for them—"

"But the rumour?" said Allison.

"I asked Whittaker to start a rumour among the players to the effect that the Yard are looking over the Stadium for a ring."

Clinton took a deep breath. Allison sat very still.

"Then you expect to catch the—"

The Arsenal manager hesitated.

"I do," said Slade.

After that there was nothing else to say. The remainder of the half-hour dragged very slowly. When a quarter of an hour had passed Slade and Clinton went out into the ground, walked about in the sunshine for a few minutes. They were aware that the men in training kit eyed them with a new interest. Somehow a feeling of crisis was in the air.

A strange, inexplicable restiveness was noticeable. As by mutual agreement, the players stopped serious training and mooched about in groups. Some went back to the dressing-rooms and sat on the seats, talking in subdued tones. Others went into the treatment room, stared round, touching nothing, and went away puzzled.

The whole of the Stadium staff seemed affected by a presentiment of something about to happen. Miss Palmer, George Allison's secretary, who usually wears a smile, looked grave as she told Slade he was wanted on the 'phone.

As he supposed, it was the Yard. A report had been received from the laboratory. Aconitine had been proved on the prised claw of the solitaire diamond ring. Slade hung up, feeling that he couldn't be wrong.

He passed on the news to Clinton. The sergeant nodded.

"Everything turning out as you thought," he said.

"We won't count our chickens too soon, Clinton."

Clinton pulled a face.

"You're not afraid of finding one's an ugly duckling, are you?"

"I shall be afraid—mortally afraid," Slade said gravely, "if I don't find an ugly duckling."

Clinton could contain himself no longer.

"But he won't fall for it! You can't expect him to. If he goes in there and searches the dish of horsehair, then he won't be fool enough to leave his finger-prints all over the sides and lid."

He seemed anxious lest, for once, his chief had slipped.

"I'm not bothering about his finger-prints, Clinton," Slade told him.

Clinton gaped, recovered himself, and said with a frown, "But how the devil can you expect to nail him if you don't get his finger-prints?"

"I'm hoping he'll give himself away."

For Clinton, it was like trying to see through a brick wall. He desisted. He was inherently suspicious of walls of any kind.

"Well, it's nice to be out in the sunshine, anyway," he said archly. "That's something I can understand."

Slade smiled.

"Sorry, Clinton, but if it doesn't work out—"

The sergeant flashed him a quick glance, and was surprised by the sudden look of strain and anxiety he discovered on Slade's face. It was as though for a brief instant the detective had lowered a shutter, and the sergeant could see inside this imperturbable man with his strong conviction and his iron purpose.

Only then did Clinton realize to the full just what the passing minutes meant to Slade.

"It'll work out," he said gruffly. "It'll have to work out. Law of averages," he added, wondering who had mentioned the term to him recently.

Slade smiled at the implied compliment, and the shutters were up again.

"Nice of you, Clinton. Thanks. Well, the half-hour's up. Let's go back and pick up our man."

Confidence rang again in the speaker's voice. It was the old Slade once more, sure of himself.

"Right. This bit of sun isn't fooling me that it's summer," Clinton rejoined, and turned on his heel.

Most of the Arsenal players were in their dressing-room by this time, while the majority of the Trojans were in the treatment room. Kindilett and Raille were a little apart, talking. Morring and Setchley stood surrounded by other players.

Slade and Clinton went into the treatment room.

"Here we are, Inspector," said Kindilett, in a voice vibrant with strain.

The door opened. Two more Trojans entered.

"That's the lot," said Clinton.

Every one watched Slade, as though he were a conjuror about to produce a rabbit from a hat.

"I'll be frank with you," said the Yard man, glancing round at his watchful audience. "I've brought you here because I think I can now place my hand on the murderer of your team-mate, John Doyce."

No one spoke. Glances narrowed, shuttlecocked, a few feet fidgeted.

Clinton felt the intangible pressure of that moment perhaps as much as anyone in that room save the murderer.

Could Slade be wrong? If he *was* wrong…

Suddenly, it seemed to the sergeant, his chief had taken too large a gamble. Distrusting the intrinsic value of purely circumstantial evidence, Slade had decided to procure something that was irrefutable. But what? How?

Slade said quietly, "I want you all to hold out your hands, palms upwards."

There was a moment's pause. Then a pair of hands was held out, and another, and a third.

"All of you—every one here," said Slade sharply.

Clinton, throwing his chief a swift glance, saw that for a moment the shutters were once more down. This was Slade's great moment of doubt.

The sergeant glanced at the semicircle of men standing with hands outstretched. He caught his breath. One pair of hands was different from the others. The fingers and palms were tinted with a pale blue deposit.

Slade jumped forward as the blue-stained hands moved. There was a quick, brief struggle, and before the startled gathering were aware of what was happening a pair of handcuffs clicked.

"My God!" murmured Francis Kindilett, staring at the handcuffs.

They were round the wrists of George Raille.

XVIII

Mystery No Longer

Halff an hour later, after Raille had left the stadium in a police-car, Slade went up to George Allison's room. The Arsenal manager was talking to Kindilett. Both men turned to the detective with looks of inquiry.

"Clinton's taken him," said Slade.

Allison said, "And now a glass of sherry, eh, Inspector?"

The sherry tasted good. Slade filled and lit his pipe, conscious that the eyes of Francis Kindilett did not leave his face.

"Did you know he was engaged to your daughter? Really know, Mr Kindilett?"

The Trojan manager shook his head.

"No. I told the truth when I said I didn't know, Inspector."

"But you suspected he might be?"

"I didn't feel free to talk about my suspicions."

Slade leaned back in his chair.

"Of course not. Perfectly reasonable. But did you have an idea he killed Doyce?"

Kindilett's face was troubled. "I didn't know what to think," he confessed. "The whole thing, it was a nightmare, and I felt afraid, not so much for myself, but for the team. I could see this horrible business ending everything. And now, without Raille, it's going to be hard. He was a remarkable man in many ways."

"Told me he wanted to be a dentist."

Kindilett looked up.

"He did? I thought he kept that a secret. Yes, I know he had great hopes of being a dental surgeon. He was studying when he was a member of the Saxon Amateurs' regular team. I never knew what made him give it up."

"I should say it was because he lost the girl he loved."

Kindilett's grey head nodded.

"You got a statement from him, didn't you, Inspector?"

"Yes. I gave him the customary warning, as you heard. When we got alone he wanted to talk. Seemed glad to get it off his chest. For years he's been hating Doyce, but he had got over the worst of it when he stumbled on the Doyce and Morring business. I'm referring to Doyce's playing around with Morring's fiancée. He could see a repetition of what happened in Ryechester four years ago. And thought of another man's happiness being ruined made him savage, and he determined to do something about it. All the old hatred for Doyce came back. And although he didn't tell me, I believe Doyce was difficult to handle. Doyce knew he had been engaged to your daughter, and he soon found out that Raille had never told you. For some reason he's shy when talking about you. I don't know why it is. Perhaps after four years he feels he wants to let the past remain buried. But I did notice that he kept from mentioning you whenever he could."

"Rather strange, isn't it?" asked Allison, leaning across his desk.

"No, I don't think so," said Slade. "Raille is a sensitive type. He hides it well, but he is all the same. Your daughter, Mr Kindilett, did not mention his name to you, and then the engagement was broken off. He felt, as I understand him, as though he didn't want you to know. If your daughter hadn't told you, then he wasn't going to. Do you follow what I mean?"

"Yes, I do," said Kindilett sadly. "Poor fellow! And did he explain to you just how Doyce managed to break up the engagement?"

"No. Again he seemed shy. And I didn't press him. He was volunteering this information, clearing his mind of a cloud, as it were. I let him tell me what he wanted to. I didn't think it the time to question him closely. He has all that to face later. But he did make it plain that what Doyce did four years ago he did wantonly, deliberately. And he did tell me to tell you that he is determined to keep your daughter's name out of the trial. He isn't afraid. He's rather the reverse. Glad it's all over."

Kindilett rose and stood looking out of the window. Slade recalled how he had stood in a similar attitude that night he had called at the hotel in Bloomsbury.

"I can hardly believe it's all happened, even now," said the Trojan manager.

"Tell me one thing," said Slade. "Was Doyce troubling you, Mr Kindilett? Making trouble, I mean, about a letter you wrote him after your daughter's death?"

Kindilett spun round, a flush in his cheeks.

"How did you know?" he asked hoarsely.

"I thought so," nodded Slade. "I've got the letter, as it happens, and I suspected that Doyce would have made himself a nuisance about it. Was his attitude vindictive?"

"Yes, that would describe it. He threatened to show it to the F.A., and say he was being victimized on account of a personal grudge if I didn't see that he was made captain in place of Chulley. I was in a difficult position."

Allison grunted. "The swine! Anything to capture the limelight for himself."

Kindilett nodded.

"Did Raille know anything about that?" asked Slade.

"I can't say. I didn't tell him. Why?"

"Oh, something he dropped rather gave me the impression that he had some other reason for disliking Doyce intensely, something to do with the team."

"It may have been that," Kindilett frowned. "It's quite possible that Doyce, knowing Raille was engaged to Mary, may have referred to the past. He could be very unpleasant—"

"Why on earth didn't you pitch him out on his ear?" said Allison indignantly. "Why stand for it?"

Kindilett smiled.

"Setchley was making quite a fuss, George. And Setchley has the backing of several people who make the Trojans possible as a financial enterprise. You know my difficulties. My hand was forced. Morring of course offered firm objection. But Setchley carried the day. Now you know." He turned to Slade again. "But why the Press cutting?"

"It was his way of telling Doyce the end had been reached. As he told me, everything seemed to happen at once to make him kill Doyce. He came across your daughter's ring, he went with you to the laboratory, and was left staring at a poison cabinet. He had to visit Doyce, and he saw the Laruce girl's handbag there. He knew it was hers—"

"We all knew her quite well," said Kindilett.

"And he left Doyce's flat on the Friday night determined to go through with it."

"But if he had taken the poison several days before," said Allison, "surely his mind didn't want making up. It was made up."

"Well, that's the whole point," said Slade. "From what he told me I gathered that he 'phoned Doyce and told him to leave the Laruce girl alone. Gave him a warning."

"Anonymously?" asked Kindilett.

"That was the impression I got," went on the Yard man.

"As if Doyce would have taken any notice!"

"Perhaps not," said Slade. "But Raille wanted to find out. So he fixed the call for Friday night. He took Doyce by surprise, and saw the handbag. That settled everything. He went through with it. Made up the parcel, pasted together the cutting, and the next morning took the package to the District Messenger's office at Victoria. After Doyce was dead he hid the ring in the bowl of horsehair. He knew where to look for it, of course. It was his plan to get the ring away later, when it wasn't dangerous, and leave the whole thing a complete mystery. He never thought it would ever be worked out. It unnerved him when he saw the possibility of Morring or yourself, Mr Kindilett, being arrested. Only then did he realize that he had something else to do. He had to make sure no one was mistakenly arrested."

"But what could he do?"

"He didn't say. I gathered that he was prepared to give himself up if the worst came to the worst."

"Well, it has," said Allison bluntly.

Kindilett sat down, lit a fresh cigarette.

"Tell me, Inspector," he requested, "when you first thought it might be Raille."

"After the inquest. I asked him to come along to the Yard. I had one or two things to ask him about the team. His manner was evasive, although he did his best to act natural. I rather stressed the case we had made out against Morring. He reacted to that immediately. In fact, the interview was a series of sharp reactions on his part."

"And that was your first suspicion?" said Allison.

"It was the first time I considered Raille seriously as a possibility. You yourself made it a certainty."

"How?" Allison was puzzled. "I remember you said something to that effect last night, but I thought you were just putting me off."

"No, I meant it," said Slade. "You brought me an album of soccer photos to look over."

Allison glanced at Kindilett. "Your album, Francis. I've got it at home, and Slade came round last night. I showed it to him."

Kindilett nodded and turned to the detective.

"You found a clue in it?"

"I did. A very valuable clue. It made the issue clear-cut."

"Is it something you can tell us at this stage?" asked the Arsenal manager.

"Oh, yes," Slade said. "Don't you remember I took out a photo of the Saxon Amateurs, or, rather, some of them. There was a note in Mr Kindilett's writing on the back."

"You mean you saw Raille in the group?"

"I saw a man with a moustache who could have been Raille four years before. I wasn't sure. I asked you if you recognized anyone there. You said no."

"True," said Allison, "I didn't recognize Raille."

"But how did you, Inspector?" asked Kindilett. "And, if I may be obtuse, how did that point to Doyce's murderer?"

"You see," Slade resumed, "I had the photo I brought back from Ryechester. That showed the same man as the Saxon Amateurs player who wore a moustache. But in the Ryechester photo he was in civvies. It wasn't difficult to link the two. And Raille was the only member of the Saxon Amateurs with the Trojans. It was a direct lead."

"Well, I missed it," Allison confessed, "and I saw both photos."

"I was wondering," said Slade, "if there wasn't some comment at the time the first photo was published in the *Ryechester Chronicle*. People four years ago would have recognized Raille, and being shown in the photo with your daughter, while the other men in the picture were members of the Rovers—well, I should have thought it would have produced some comment."

"Gossip, Inspector, gossip," said Kindilett, pulling a wry face. "The town was full of talk. Mary was engaged in turn to half the population of the borough. Then it died down."

Slade nodded. "I see. I was wondering if you hadn't yourself got some vague idea, at least, about Raille from the photograph."

"Honestly I can't say I had, Inspector. The whole thing was a great shock to me. I—I'm afraid that Raille, despite his good intentions, won't be able to keep Mary's name out of the trial when it comes on. I don't see that it is possible. Do you?"

He looked hopefully at the detective, but Slade, who had been troubled by the same doubt himself, shook his head.

"I didn't say so just now, but frankly I don't see how he can. The Prosecution will build part of its case, the greater part in fact, on what happened back in Ryechester. Motive begins there."

Kindilett sighed.

"As I thought, Inspector. It was too much to hope that he would be able to prevent the inevitable."

"Well, of course, it's not the inevitable, exactly," said Slade. "But it depends on how a defence counsel will advise him to plead, and how the defence is constructed. One can never tell, naturally."

Allison tried to turn the conversation into a less painful channel.

"How were you so sure he would come for the ring?"

"I told Clinton the way to catch our man was to mix self-preservation, curiosity, and sentiment. Self-preservation—well, we don't need to look hard at that. It wouldn't be human not to try to kill Doyce without at the same time hoping to go free. Curiosity. There again Raille reacted as I expected. He wanted to know what the police had found, and that rumour of a ring would have told him something was discovered. He wouldn't know how much, but the urge to find out would grow. It became allied with self-preservation."

"Yes, I can see that," nodded the Arsenal manager.

"Then sentiment." Slade paused. "He used his engagement ring because it was symbolic of—oh, poetic justice, if you like. The ring returned to him, the ring he had kept as a tragic memento. You see how it could have seemed to him. But he also cherished that ring for what it had originally stood for. He would want it back. Thought of the police finding it and probably throwing it in a drawer or file—well, that irked him. Sentiment."

Slade wasn't sure whether or not Kindilett was listening. His gaze was far-away. But Allison was following the detective's words closely.

He had another question ready, one he had been saving since he had heard of Raille's arrest.

"Just how did you trick him, Inspector? What did you use?"

Slade smiled. "Bromophenol," he said. "It's a yellowish substance which when mixed with the perspiration on one's hands turns blue. I knew it wouldn't be any good waiting to get fingerprints. Our man would be too fly to leave any. He'd wipe the glass after touching the bowl and the lid. But by that time the powder would be on his hands. He wouldn't notice it, and his hands would be moist. A fairly safe assumption, for he was bound to be worked up, excited. Especially when he discovered that the ring wasn't there. He'd know then that the trick was seen through."

"That's what I don't understand," said Allison, "why he hid it just where he did."

"I think that's clear now," said Slade. "When the treatment room was left open he could come in any time and no one would object or even notice him if he took a piece of horsehair from the jar. Would seem the natural thing for him to do. He was the Trojan trainer, after all. So that, basically, his choice of hiding-place was sound."

Allison nodded.

"Yes, I see the point now, Inspector. Ingenious fellow, really."

Slade glanced at Kindilett, and made no rejoinder.

"How about the rest of the poison—" Allison began, when the 'phone rang stridently.

He unhooked it.

"Hallo. Yes? Oh. For you, Inspector."

Slade moved round the desk and took the receiver.

"Who is it?" he asked.

"Clinton," said a voice he recognized. "I've got some news."

The sergeant's excited tones crackled in the receiver, so that Slade had to hold it farther from his ear. But the sergeant could be forgiven his excitement. He really had news.

Slade put down the receiver, and turned to Kindilett.

"That story won't be told in court, Mr Kindilett," he said.

Kindilett started.

"I—What, Inspector? Won't be told? But you said—"

Slade shook his head.

"I'm afraid George Raille himself won't be appearing in court," he added. "He's dead. And there is a fresh pin-prick in his right wrist."

"Good God!" Allison exclaimed.

Kindilett stood very still. Slade watched him.

"So he meant it. He meant it," he repeated to himself. "That was the last thing he could do for her."

There was a great wonder in his voice.

Slade turned to the Arsenal manager. "There is no more mystery, Mr Allison, and I think your last question is answered—at least, in part."

Allison nodded.

"Yes, I agree, Inspector," he said. He glanced inquiringly at the Yard man, who nodded.

They went out of the room, leaving Kindilett staring out of the window and seeing nothing, a grey-haired man alone with his thoughts.